# Time and Time Again

A Novel by:

Bill Trumble

This book is dedicated to Mayme and Jonathan.

# CONTENTS

Preface                                                    1

Chapt. 1  **The end of a normal life**                     5

Chapt. 2  **Lost**                                         19

Chapt. 3  **Night in the Alzheimer's ward**               41

Chapt. 4  **Rimu's Story: Tenaru**                         58

Chapt. 5  **The Joys of Administration**                   89

Chapt. 6  **Rimu's Story: McMurdock's Folly**             99

Chapt. 7  **Back at the Geezer Garage**                   114

Chapt. 8  **Orb wars and the Forbidden Pass**             125

Chapt. 9  **I should have retired**                       146

Chapt. 10  **New Directions**                             158

Chapt. 11  **Out of my mind**                             173

Chapt. 12  **Time and time again**                        177

Postscript                                                199

# Preface

I tell people that my Dad has Alzheimer's disease, but it is worse than that. He sits in a chair not moving by day, and lies not moving in bed by night. Well, that's not entirely correct since he moves his fingers – only his fingers. When we found him, after what the doctors suggested might have been a stroke, he was sitting up typing on his computer in the camper on his pickup truck. The computer wasn't plugged in and the batteries were stone dead, yet my Dad was typing away though no letters were being displayed. He has been effectively paralyzed since that day and has never spoken audibly since. His mouth hints at making words, but even if that were the case, no sounds comes out and although he may have tried to communicate often, he has not been heard or made contact with anyone for two years.

My name is Jonathan Hart, but I go by Jon. My Dad is Dr. Al Hart, a biochemist who worked for 30 years at Utopia University in Idaho. Dad was relatively well known for his research and teaching until two years ago when we found him unable to move. He was reputed by his colleagues to have a nearly a photographic memory (a gene he did not, regrettably, pass on to me), but now he has been diagnosed with Catatonic Dementia. It doesn't help much to look it up; I tried, but the term is so non-descript that I now consider it one of those labels for maladies where no definitive definition exists. In his case, it simply means he can't move – except his fingers.

I can't imagine what being place-bound and paralyzed means to my Dad. He was an extraordinary outdoorsman and one of those handy types. I was impressed, even when I was younger, by how there was almost nothing that he couldn't do – build a room on the house, fix a car, craft a guitar, sequence a gene, or type a bacterial culture. Since my Mom died of cancer ten years ago, he has been a single Dad and my main mentor. He got me through college, leaving me the gift of being without school debts, and ever since I've been trying to run a small water-testing laboratory I started in Oregon. But my personal debt to my Dad runs deeper than anyone understands and so I put the water lab on hold for six months to be with him when he came home from the hospital after what is most often called a "stroke". Following those six months, when I found that I could do nothing more for him, I went back to Oregon for the last year and a half. But now I'm looking to move the water-testing lab to Spokane, WA or maybe Coeur d'Alene, ID, so I can be with him more. Something has happened recently of which, for now, I am (I think) the only one aware. You are about to experience an incredible story, written by the person to whom it appears to have happened. If any of it is true, the implications are stunning.

Isn't it amazing that everything we sense, experience, think or observe is processed through our brains? Indeed, reality is the result of this processing. If something doesn't come through our brains, well, it didn't happen for us. We have all had extremely realistic dreams. How real are they? It is worth noting that our body is effectively paralyzed when we are in deep sleep to protect us from doing something that could harm us as we experience what seems entirely real in those dreams. The message to take home from this is that if your brain processes an experience, it is real to you at the time. The real question is whether our minds are just the faithful reporters of events or can they create the program that we see as reality? I remember the fictional movie "The Matrix", where almost all of humanity was programmed to process a modified "reality" through their minds, rather than what was actually real. Maybe the premise was correct.

Who knows what goes on in the mind of an Alzheimer patient, or what goes on in my Dad's mind, for that matter, as he sits virtually frozen and types on his computer? Are those patient's minds aware of the immediate present, or are they in another "reality" created by their mind? Do they think, or dream, or just sit vacant? Well, now I have a hint, and that is why I am returning to be with my Dad.

During the first six months after the onset of his Catatonic Dementia, I wanted my Dad in physical therapy, to preserve his muscle tone. But he couldn't move and thus could not help the process and the therapist held out little hope, despite my insisting on this therapy. While I was planning to return to the water lab in Oregon after being with Dad for six months and not able to communicate, I remembered that when we found my Dad, he was going though the motions of typing. The staff in the Alzheimer's ward of the nursing home and I finally settled on a protocol such that they would have him seated each morning at a computer (I got him a new Mac laptop with mega-memory and an automatic "save" program) and hopefully he would continue to type and not lose the use of his fingers – the only part of his body that moved. A month ago, mechanical failure caused the keyboard on the computer to freeze up and need replacing. The Alzheimer's ward staff packed up the machine and sent it to me in Oregon. I had the built-in laptop keyboard replaced and when the machine was working, I spent an evening - out of curiosity - (and then the next two full days) looking at what was on the computer. Needless to say, I expected random letters with no content or focus, if anything. But I was wrong! The story you are about to read is the story my Dad typed during the last year and a half.

Tomorrow, I'm flying to Spokane with the computer. In the weeks since the computer broke, I am concerned that I am missing the next chapter of my Dad's story. I'm even holding out hope there is now a way to communicate with him, during one phase of the two lives he now seems to be living. At the very least, I can assure you that I have no concern that my Dad's mind is vacant. One part of what he has written I know to be based in fact, because I've heard some version of these stories before. Another part is beyond my knowledge and even my imagination. How much is real? I really don't know, but hope to find out. For now, you will have to decide for yourself if what you read is real.

# Chapter 1

## The end of a normal life

Hey Folks, a little help here, please. Damn it, at least talk to me. Something has happened to me and I'm stranded in some sort of old folks home, unable to move. Everything I do, except type, seems to take forever; an hour to say even a sound, minutes to move my eyes, a day to move my foot an inch. But my mind has not slowed down at all. I understand what I see or hear, but since I can't respond quickly enough, people have given up on me. I'm moved daily between two positions, one at a table with the computer and other in a bed, and once positioned I might as well be on the moon as no one interacts with me since they think that I can't respond.

What happened to me? I catch phrases and parts of sentences from others talking about me and hear discussions of "strokes", Alzheimer's, and dementia - but these sentences are never directed at me, but to someone else about me. And why do my fingers work but not the rest of me, and why doesn't someone read this if they are going to put me at a computer? I'm going to lose it and go crazy if I can't communicate with someone. I've apparently been here (wherever "here" is) for some time prior to now, but large blocks of time are missing from my memory. So I've decided to document what is happening, using the only parts of me that I still control – fingers and mind, and this computer. Probably this is just an exercise to keep from going mad, and it may indeed be too late. But something is going on that I certainly don't understand. Did I drive myself crazy? Is this what happens if you blow up your brain working a crazy job? Well, I have some speculations, but no real answers, so I'm going to try to capture what is going on in what is left of my mind. The more I write (and read) of my own story, the more I think I'm beginning to understand something of my situation. So here goes:

The last things I can remember about what I will call my "normal" life are the camping trip and the brilliant, silent, and intensely white light. Not the warm, inviting light that is suppose to welcome you to death; this light built from nothing in the dark of night to great intensity in milliseconds, much as I would imagine would happen in the middle of a nuclear explosion. Indeed, the very last "normal" thought I recall was the question whether I was witnessing an atomic bomb blast up close and personal. Yet there was no sound, no impact, and no heat – just white, white light.

But I am getting ahead of myself. Let me start a little earlier in the memory of my time (if time has any meaning), so you can understand who I am, something of the normal life I have lost, and how it has come to be that I write these words. I'm effectively paralyzed and, as best I can tell, only four parts of my body still work: my brain (which is totally aware and remembers everything about my past life, but nothing about what seems to be a current part of my life), my fingers (including my thumbs), my eyes (which focus instantly but move side to side or up and down only very, very slowly), and a swallowing reflex when stuff is put in my mouth. I assume some waste processing must still function, but I can't actually be sure since I have no feeling and apparently no sense of smell. I have a total movement range of nine inches per hand, from the tip of my little finger to the end of my thumb. And I blame that damn white light – but I'll get to that soon enough. My fingers and my brain are all that I control and are my only hope for sanity, escape from this mental prison, and any hope of communication. The computer is my lifeline - if someone will read what I put on it.

I've rearranged, from memory, the information I am writing to allow me to start this story with my normal life, before I found myself in this hospital, or old folks home, or wherever it is I'm now living (using the term "living" rather loosely). A short history of the me that I know might be helpful to give you some perspective on why I don't consider myself crazy, and then I'll relate the stories that have clearly been written by me about events that have apparently occurred to me, but of which I remember nothing.

I'm 57 years old and for 20 years I was a professor and scientific researcher. The next 13 years I was involved mostly in university administration. My area is (was) biochemistry and microbiology, with a medical and agricultural focus. I was lucky enough to have been trained in the techniques of molecular biology in the 1970s, when I was a student, as the techniques were being developed, and, largely as a function of being in the right place at the right time, many of the experiments I conducted turned out to be important just because no one had been able to do them prior to the development of new molecular techniques. So I enjoyed the privilege of being invited to share my results with scientists all over the world. And while I traveled, engrossed in my own success, a cancer was growing unknown in my wife. She would die the day following our 20th anniversary. I was left without my best friend (with the realization that I would trade all my scientific recognition to have her back) and as the single parent to a 15-year old son, Jon. (I'm sure Jon is responsible for setting me up with this computer; someday I intend to figure out how to ask him what the heck took him so long to read the files).

The death of my wife upset my perfect world, and my need to be the sole provider for my son led me to accept a more lucrative offer to move from teaching and research to university administration. What would I give for the chance to do my life over? I'd give almost anything; except perhaps finding myself back in the non-moving hell that I am now living. I'd concentrate on being the best teacher my students ever had; I'd do some research, but limit my travel; I'd pay a lot more attention to my wife and family; and I'd avoid university administration like the plague. My normal life is now gone, along with half of my family, but I don't face despair since I've apparently been given the gift of another particularly fantastic life. Again, I'm getting ahead of myself; so let me start at the beginning with the end of my normal life.

Each year it had become my habit to go camping and fishing over the date of my wife's death. For several years I took my son, but he was at an age when he wanted to be with his friends and I came to realize that the purpose of the trip was really for me to get away where I could remember and grieve without the need to explain. She had died on October 12th and some years it can be really cold in October in northern Idaho, though most years the weather is wonderful and Indian summers make it a delight to be outdoors. It was that way, beautiful, when I packed to take two weeks vacation. Jon had moved to Oregon a couple of years earlier and my only responsibility was my dog, River, who always went camping with me. I've gotten lazy as old age approached, and come to enjoy certain luxuries, so I always packed far too much to backpack into my favorite location. I had always carried a little "medicinal" brandy when I backpacked to take away the pains after a long hike (well worth its weight), but this annual trip was embellished with a single malt scotch, a six pack of beer, full fishing tackle for spinning and fly rods, warm and cold weather gear, a satellite phone (that I've never used, but made sure my son had the number), tools (ax, saw, rope) and a white-gas camp stove and white-gas lantern, a 38 caliber pistol that I had inherited from my Father, and an industrial sized first-aid kit (to which I was always adding new creams, antibiotics, sterile pads, and painkillers, seldom taking anything out, and leaving the legality of its contents highly questionable). After trips to Nepal and several other remote locations, my first aid kit rivaled a bad pharmacy in a poor town. As you might infer, I had always lived well for those two-week camping retreats and never lost a pound despite being pretty active.

To move this mountain of junk, I took my 9-foot aluminum flat-bottom boat to serve the purpose of a pack mule. Each summer, as I fished Marble Creek on any number of weekends, I would move boulders, limbs, and logs to ensure a channel that would let me walk along the shore and float my camping-gear-loaded boat the four and eight-tenths miles along the creek to a grassy meadow bordered on one side by the Marble Creek and on the other side by a small lake. A densely wooded hill came down to the unnamed lake on three sides, so access was difficult except by following the creek. The meadow was a fisherman's secluded paradise. The clear, quick running creek and the deep lake offered the best possible fishing and exquisite wildlife viewing. It is a place that makes one's heart sing. After unloading the boat, the plan would be to drag it across the meadow to use on the small lake.

Leaving the University early on a Friday, I loaded my gear into my 10-year old, 4-wheel drive truck that looked every minute of its age. The truck was rigged with a camper that fit in the truck bed and a mechanical crank that let me wench the boat up onto the top of the camper (I told you I'd gotten lazy). The packs, boxes of food, and tools went in the back seat of the extended cab or on the floor of the camper. As usual, my dog River occupied the truck's passenger seat. Since I had the camper, it wouldn't matter what time of day (or night) I arrived at the site where I would put my boat into Marble Creek, so by 4:00pm I was driving the two and one half hours north and east into the Idaho panhandle. In Idaho, short of going to the Frank Church Wilderness, the Marble Creek area was about as remote as one could get. I was confident I would see no other humans for the next two weeks.

Several rustic campsites exist off old logging roads bordering sections of Marble Creek. One particularly rough and uninviting track leads to three tent sites with one beat up picnic table. After squeezing the truck into the site that is my favorite, because it let me look across the creek to a wide grassy field edged by pines, I set up to spend the night in the camper and get an early start up Marble Creek in the morning. River and I explored the camp area and the creek while it was light, returned to the camper to fix a quick dinner, and I settled in with a book and a beer before turning in to sleep by 10:30pm.

Now, I know better than to have a beer just before going to sleep. Beer runs though me like water through a strainer. But damn if it doesn't just taste better when one is relaxing in anticipation of a great time. However, as I could have predicted, about 1:45am I was standing just outside the camper relieving myself. I could have used the camper's toilet but then I would be faced later with having to empty the holding tank, and this was just a one-night-stay before that luxury would be no longer available anyway. It was a cloudless night; the moon was more than three quarters full and there was enough ambient light that dark-accustomed eyes could see shadows. From inside the camper, River gave a low growl and at that moment the moonlight reflected like fire off some large animal's pair of yellow eyes. Even after a lifetime in the woods, something like that always gave me the chills and made the hair stand up on the back of my neck. I reached back in the camper for my flashlight and in seconds had the flashlight beam on the spot where the eyes had been. There was nothing there. From the safety of the door of the camper, I searched the dark cave-like shadows of the woods with my light. But nothing was visible, nothing was moving, River was calm and quiet, and the jolt of adrenaline that had caused my hair to stand on end began its slow process of wearing off.

River and I were up and out of the camper early and, as we did every day, spent the first half hour in training exercises. River was a rescued police dog. After working over a year and a half as a Seattle police K-9, his partner/handler was killed by a gang member in a senseless shooting. The 85-pound German shepherd-Lab mix would not accept another police handler and was put up for adoption. One of my old college buddies, now an active police officer, thought I needed a dog for company, since this was some years after the death of my wife, and brought the dog over to Idaho to meet me. We hit it off immediately, and that was that. We have been spending a half hour in dog training every morning for 4 or 5 years. River expects it and I like knowing that I can count on River if ever I should need help. It is quality bonding-time for both of us.

Once, long ago, I had a friend who had a St. Bernard. Needless to say, this was a big dog; but it was also in great shape at more than a hundred and twenty pounds of solid muscle with the biggest mouth I'd ever seen on a dog. On a walk with my friend and his dog, I watched a smaller dog that was "on-the-loose" challenge the St. Bernard and could see by the posture of both dogs that a fight was imminent. I was sure the smaller dog was toast, but without raising his voice my friend called his dog to "come" and the St. Bernard immediately backed away from the smaller dog without breaking eye contact and came to sit by my friend. I chased off the smaller dog, but always thought my friend's dog was the most well trained dog I'd ever seen. But that was before I'd worked with River. Now, I'd stand him against any dog or pig anywhere ("that'll do River"). I can't take the credit though; the police folks trained him before I got him, and for the first year he was with us it was my son, Jon, who worked with him more than I did. I just continued working with the dog when Jon finished college and went to Oregon.

Sunrise had brought the promise of warmth and spectacular weather for the last day of my normal life. Still feeling the chill from seeing the mysterious eyes the night before, and since the campsite was empty save for my truck, I dug through the boxes and pulled out a holster and the pistol and strapped them to my belt. The two clips with the bullets were housed in a separate case on my belt, so, while the gun was unloaded, ammunition was easily accessible. Despite feeling somewhat like a wimp for having gotten out the gun, I was somehow comforted by it's weight as I slipped the boat into the creek and loaded the gear. River knew this drill, load the boat and then off to the wilderness. He couldn't have been happier and to make sure that I didn't leave him, he jumped into the front of the boat, sitting with his head high, more than a little bit resembling George Washington crossing the Delaware. He carried most of the food he would eat in a dog-vest with a dozen pockets. Once underway, I was sure the dog would stay in the boat probably less than two minutes; there were woods to explore. Without bothering to lock the truck, I started walking up the creek towing the "mule-boat". The mountain-men of old would have thought I was crazy.

The trip up-river was leisurely and easy most of the way. I had to move only a couple of rocks and one blown down tree limb to get the boat past rough spots, but the easy travel was more a testament to my clearing efforts over the summer while I fished than to the natural state of the creek. I stopped twice to fish for about a half hour each time and once to let River harass a raccoon. At about four miles in, with roughly a mile remaining to get to our destination, the boat hit an obstacle I hadn't seen from the edge of the creek. It was a particularly shallow area where the bottom was almost as visible as if the water had not been there, yet the clear, rippling creek appeared to offer sufficient depth for the flat-bottomed boat to float easily.

After walking fully around the boat and seeing nothing that seemed to be holding up our progress, I let the current take the boat a few feet downstream and tied it to a tree, giving instructions to River to watch the boat and associated stuff. Then I again walked the shore of the stream to where the boat had met resistance, looking for the obstacle. It was just after noon with the sun's rays coming almost straight down; one could see every pebble and stone on the bottom through the clear water, but nothing that would stop passage of the boat. I recalled a few choice swear words from my Navy days to express frustration at myself and went back to untie the boat and drag it past this shallow section. Again, at what appeared to be the same location, the boat ground to a stop, this time with an audible scraping noise. From the shore, I marked the spot with a small limb and for a second time let the boat drift back down stream. Once the boat was secured, I waded out into the creek once more to find the obstruction, this time sure that it really was there.

What I found was a hole in the water. Seriously, there was a hole in the creek where there was, or appeared to be, no water. From the side, the hole was not visible; only when looking directly down on the spot could one see through what appeared to be a cylindrical hole to the bottom of the creek, with no interference from water. It was the strangest thing I'd ever seen. I'd taken off my boots and socks to wade into the calf-deep area of the stream to find the obstruction, and some sharp rocks were making my movements slow. But once spotting this weird "hole", I called River over to check it out. I had wondered if there was a smell or sound he could detect, but either because he was less cautious or more curious, he dipped his head under the water and came up with the "hole" in his teeth. River held a sphere about the size of a small orange, made of something that looked like the thinnest glass possible. The creek below now ran without a hole. Since the sphere appeared to be something River had no trouble holding in his mouth, I had him drop the sphere into my hand. It appeared infinitely fragile and almost without weight. I slowly lowered it into the creek and instantly the hole reappeared in the water and the sphere itself was again invisible. When I pulled the sphere back out of the water, I was stunned to see it was not wet. Not a drop of water adhered anywhere on the sphere. Nothing I had ever seen looked or acted like this sphere. I began to think about experiments my colleagues at Utopia University could do on this oddity, but I wondered if I could get through the next two weeks without accidently breaking it. I took the pistol from its holster and put it into one of the cargo pockets on my pants and put the sphere in the holster. The flap just covered the sphere and fastened easily. At least now it couldn't fall out of the holster to its destruction; I'd just need to use enough care not to smash it against something.

The rest of the trip to the meadow and pond was uneventful and we were there in what seemed like the blink of an eye, probably because my mind was fixated on the strange sphere. Once River and I arrived at the meadow, our first priority should have been to set up camp. Instead, I spent hours just looking at the darn sphere. I wanted to examine it before it got dark, but finally had to put it aside in order to set up the tent and make some food. I'd expected to empty the boat and drag it across the meadow to the lake before dark, but ended up that evening just turning the boat upside down over most of my supplies. What the heck, I had two weeks to get everything sorted out.

I just had time to finish dinner, check my fishing gear, move the sphere to a net pocket built into the side of my tent and replace the pistol in its holster before night fell. On a lark, and because I had the boat to use as a mule, I had left only two beers in the camper for my return, and brought the three remaining beers from the six-pack to the meadow. I accepted that I would need to get up in the night, got out a beer, put River's bed by the tent door (nearest the boat so he could let me know if any marauders tried to get our stuff), and spent 45-minutes talking to River (who is a great listener and almost never interrupts), checking the dog for ticks, and nursing my beer.

The beer-timer on my bladder gave me until 2:15am before the call of nature was too strong for sleep. Sliding out of my sleeping bag in just my underwear, I felt the chill of the night air. My intent was to make a very quick trip outside and get back in the warm bag as quickly as possible. This time, I decided to take my flashlight with me and, as I searched the tent pocket where I always keep the flashlight, I noticed what appeared to be a very faint glow from, or near, the sphere. I decided I could multitask, so I slid the flashlight into the waistband of my shorts, gently grabbed the sphere and took it with me outside, leaving the tent-flap open for the minute it would take to do what I needed. Clouds covered the moon at that moment and the night was as black as only places with no light pollution can be. I braced myself against the side of the boat. As I was getting rid of the beer, I looked into the sphere to see a star-scape of the faintest lights imaginable. During the day, the sphere appeared to be entirely clear and empty but now held what looked like all the stars of the night sky, but as dim as vision allows to be seen.

At that point two things happened at once. First, having finished my business, I reached for my flashlight (tucked in the waistband of my boxer shorts) but my right hand never even reached the light's handle, only inches away. Second, a white light emanated from the sphere in my left hand, growing to an intensity that made me think I was in the middle of a nuclear bomb blast. In the microsecond of growing intensity, before only light could be seen, my mind registered one sight - as if caught in a strobe light. Half way across the creek, a large cougar was frozen in mid-jump. Its trajectory would land it six feet from a deer grazing down the meadow next to the creek, not even thirty yards from the tent. I could see that each saw the other in the light before nothing could be seen, but neither appeared to move a muscle before the light was too intense to see anything at all.

I had no idea what the light was, or what it meant. Perhaps it was a form of sudden death, perhaps an alien abduction; all sorts of possibilities have come to me after the fact, but the only thing I could think of at the time was that the eyes I had seen from the camper the night before were the eyes of that cougar. It must have followed River and me as we walked to the meadow, biding its time. I suppose River looked like a lunch and I looked like a dinner. Thank Goodness that the cougar's interest was on the deer tonight, but in any case, if we would have remained at this camp for two more weeks, one can be sure the cougar would have been hungry at some point and I hate to think of the big cat putting River or me on the menu.

The intensity of the cold, white light forced my eyes

closed. I waited for some sound or impact, but none occurred. With no sense of time, the light faded. I first checked to see if I was intact or damaged and then checked on River. He had bounded out of the tent as the light began and was standing with his shoulder against my leg. We both seemed to be all right. The tent and the boat were there and seemed unharmed. I still held the sphere; it was not broken or hot and it emitted no light now at all. Everything appeared to have come through the intense light experience in good shape. But something was wrong, and it took several minutes for me to realize what it was. It was now daytime. My watch still said 2:19am and the flashlight was still in the waistband of my underwear, but it was daylight and the sun was up.

In the daylight, it was easy to recognize why it seemed that something was not right – the creek was not there, nor was the pond. There was no wooded hill coming down to the meadow. The tent sat in a forest with no pines but with ferns and unusual trees, the tent stakes that had been driven into the grass of the meadow now lay flat on dirt, and the level, comfortable floor of the tent was sitting over an enormous root from a strange tree.

Although not very original, I reached down to pet River and said, "Toto, I don't think we are in Kansas anymore". At that point, I had no idea where I was, or that my normal life had just ended.

# Chapter 2

## Lost

*I have absolutely no memory of the following story or any of the stories from after the time when the white light burst from the sphere. I read them, as you will (I hope), as a reader living the stories vicariously. At first, I thought someone had written them on my computer while I slept, but the words and phrasing are mine, as are the interactions with my dog - including actions and commands that only I (or Jon, my son) would know. I've concluded that I wrote these stories about something I was part of, although I have no memory of them and no recollection of any of the events, or about something I dreamed in recurrent dreams. These stories are in the order I found them on my computer, but seem to have been an altogether unrecognizable, incredible, and unimaginable new experience that may have occurred only in my mind — but I don't really know.*

"River, come!" My command sounded a little sharper than I had intended. The dog was more agitated than I was, and had begun whining, sniffing and circling the area, so I talked to him to steady both of us. "Stay here, boy. Let's check our gear and then see if we can find out how we got ourselves lost. I can't imagine we're too far from our campsite, but where the hell is the creek?" I said, wondering why I was talking out loud. It may have been that I was in some sort of shock, but I went on talking aloud, "Why don't I recognize where we are or any of these trees? What the hell! Well, we've got two weeks worth of food and if we can figure out which way to go, we can walk home in two weeks". River was a good listener and it always helped me to talk through things.

All our gear seemed to be intact and nothing obvious was missing. There was no reason to panic, but a discomfort from knowing I was probably lost began to sweep over me. The discomfort was only exaggerated by the questions with no answers. How did we lose a night without realizing it? Where was the creek? Where were we? What the hell happened? Was there a cougar? Was it still nearby? What was that light? Still, there were no answers at the moment and sitting doing nothing sure didn't seem like a good idea. I decided a good start would be to get dressed.

After putting on some clothes, I moved the tent to a level area and drove the stakes into the ground. Anything that didn't seem to need the protection of being zipped in the tent was put under the boat. Wherever we were, this site would be the new base camp and I determined to explore east (toward where the truck should have been), and to note distance and compass heading in a notebook as we went. But first, there was one long shot chance at finding our way out of this that I was willing to try first. The truck was our "home away from home" and River knew the command "back to the truck". So I gave the command and put our fate in his ability to find his own scent and follow it back. Ten circles later, each with an increasing radius, River sat down indicating that there was no scent and he didn't have a clue which way was "back". I pulled out the compass, located east, and indicated to River that we would go that way.

The landscape was beautiful in a way with which I was not familiar. The trees were tall, with a great distance from the ground to the first branches, and a high canopy that blocked much of the direct sun, but not the light. The walking was easy since there was little harsh underbrush, mostly just ferns, and relatively long distances could be viewed as one looked among the tree trunks. Meadows were frequent and contained lush green grass. But after two hours of walking, carefully leaving blaze marks on trees to mark our way, we saw no paths, no roads, and no houses. More importantly, we saw no water. We would need another two hours to return to our camp and I had estimated it was near two in the afternoon when we had left the camp to explore. I particularly wanted to note what time the sun went down so I could reset my watch (my watch still said it was morning). Besides, I was tired from getting very little sleep the night before. We would try again tomorrow and go west with a full day to explore.

Back at our camp nothing had been disturbed, but I noted that what was only a chill on the night before the white light had now become downright cold as the sun went down. Fortunately, I'd packed a warm jacket. The forest was not the only thing unfamiliar now since the sky had no constellations I could recognize and there was a grouping of stares that looked like the Southern Cross. I'd seen the Southern Cross when I'd traveled to Australia and New Zealand once years ago, but I know it is not visible from the North American continent so I had no idea what I was looking at. In any case, River and I didn't spend much time looking at the night sky but rather slept the sleep of the very tired. Morning broke late for us, but clear, cool, and sunny. If we didn't find out where we were this day, we would certainly hope to find water. I made some instant oatmeal for me and fed River. Then it was off to find where the hell we were. This time we went west. I recorded our route and blazed some trees as a precaution. Two hours later it was clear we were heading toward some mountains and the density of the trees was lessening. But we had not run across a single stream or water source and I was beginning to have some concern. River and I went another two hours going west before turning back to the camp. At our most westerly point I could see the mountains curving off ahead of us to the north, and determined that the next day we would head north – hoping the mountains would increase our chance of finding water.

We were almost at our camp on the way back from our day's exploring when River stopped in his tracks; it was clear he was listening intently. It was just dusk and darkness was coming soon, but it was still light enough to see whatever had gotten River's attention. As the dog began a slow crawl forward, I was pretty sure something was waiting for us at our camp. I loaded the pistol and slowly moved forward. I didn't hear a sound, but I'd learned to trust the dog without question when he acted this way. After a couple of minutes of sneaking up to the camp, we could see a thin man, or perhaps a boy, standing just outside the perimeter of our camp on the south side. He had on green overalls of some strange material, with no shirt and no shoes. The sun had been warm in the afternoon, but with the wild temperature swings when the sun went down, it was too cold now for me to be dressed like that. He carried a stick, but I couldn't tell if it was a spear or a walking stick. I was delighted to see someone, but was still concerned that he appeared to watching our camp – maybe with a spear. I decided to confront him. I had both a pistol and River, and he only had a stick, but he seemed clearly at home here and was clearly observing our camp. As we watched, he neither moved to touch anything nor entered our camp. As I debated whether to allow River to be seen when I confronted the man, or keep the dog in reserve as my private Calvary, the man turned sharply to look to the south (not at me). He took several steps south to a clearing and stared before turning and running north past our camp at a rapid pace. Neither River nor I had made a sound and I doubt he knew we were present; but he ran deliberately as if chased by something.

I knew River could track him so I didn't try to run after him, and I wanted to see what had caused him to run away so abruptly. I slipped forward and several yards south and looked across the meadow at which he had been staring. To my amazement, a green line a foot wide was sweeping across the floor of the forest at just about a fast walking speed. How it penetrated the canopy of the trees, if it did, I had no idea, but the man or boy we had just seen clearly didn't seem to want this green line to catch him, and it occurred to me that his actions suggested River and I might not want it to catch us either. But we could either run like the thin man, that would cause us to abandon our camp to stay ahead of the green line, or try to hide from it. But we had only a minute, perhaps two at the most, before it would be at our camp. I had no idea whether to be afraid of the green line or not, but as much as I didn't want to be pushed away from our camp, I knew the man had run from it and I didn't want to chance having it touch River or me. Almost without thinking, I pulled the boat off of some gear that it had covered and turned it upside down on a clear spot. I called River and we both climbed under the boat to let the green line pass. As we hunkered down under the boat, it occurred to me that I really didn't know if the green line was coming down from the sky or up from the ground.

If it were coming up from the ground, then being under the boat was not going to be much protection from whatever it was. But it was now too late to do anything but wait for the line to pass by us. My hope was that the boat would shield us from the green line. So it seemed logical that, since we were hiding under the boat, if we saw the green line cross us then 1) the line must come from the ground and we would be exposed to it or 2) it came from above and the boat had offered no protection, in which case the green line had gone right through the boat and we would be exposed to it. Only if the line came from above and we did not see it cross over us while we huddled under the boat could we hope to have been protected from whatever it was. For a very long number of seconds we waited for the line to cross past us. During that time I thought about the boat we were hiding under. The damn boat had been recently painted in camouflage colors and I hate camouflage.

The short story was that I had loaned the boat to a longtime neighbor, who had used it on a couple of previous occasions, for duck hunting. This guy was one of the world's most avid duck hunters and had used my little boat at a time when his boat was undergoing repairs for some reason during duck season. He had been especially successful on that outing and as a "thank you" to me had hand-painted the boat in his garage, applying multiple coats of the very best marine paint he could get. The paint job was really a work of art, particularly so since my boat looked like crap when l let him use it. Now the only thing (hopefully) between River and me and the green line was my newly painted, camouflage colored, aluminum boat. I found myself hoping that my neighbor had used lead-based paint in case there was any radiation associated with the green line.

To my amazement, the green line passed over the boat and we did not see it on the ground below the boat. Perhaps the boat had protected us, or perhaps the green line didn't have any effect, but it appears the line had come from above and had not penetrated the boat. Maybe the green line would not have penetrated the tent, but I decided to use the boat to create a lean-to under which we could hide from the green line until I could do an experiment to see if the tent was sufficient to provide protection as well. Not knowing when the green line might come again, we moved our beds (sleeping bag) under the boat for the night. It was my intention to have River track the thin man in the morning when we could see clearly, and the fact that he had run north meant I didn't have to change our intent to go north as well. The fact that someone might be living around here was the first good news we'd had since the intense light came out of that damn sphere.

I slept a pretty fitful night wondering if the man might return, and both River and I were ready to leave camp by just after daybreak. If River was going to be tracking the thin man, that seemed like a good enough exercise to substitute for our morning training session. I had granola for breakfast, with beer instead of powdered milk (to save the water we had), and found it is not as bad as one would have guessed. Then we immediately started after the running man. I took only the pistol, a water bottle and some food (for both River and I) in a daypack, and the sphere. Somehow, I had convinced myself the sphere was involved with our current situation and I was not about to become separated from it yet. River had little trouble, with a few false starts, following the trail of the man we sought; however, our progress was painfully slow. The running man had apparently continued to run a good distance after leaving our camp since, after tracking him for three hours and covering some good number of miles, we saw no evidence that the man stopped to sleep - or that we were getting any closer to finding him. As we crept ahead, a memory returned to me of reading about a native tribe in South America where tribe members ran barefoot and could run for 24 hours without stopping. It would be just my luck to have the guy we were following able to do something like that. We hadn't brought gear to continue the search beyond a day, and if we didn't find the runner, River and I would have to return to camp for food and drink, decide what to take and what to leave if we wanted to search longer for the elusive runner, and accept the fact that the trail would be a day older. It didn't escape my mind that, while River just went about tracking sure he would eventually find whom he was seeking, I was conjuring up the most negative thoughts I could invent. Maybe that had something to do with what success I had seen as a scientist; I always seemed to dwell on the negative and had to prove to myself any data, idea, or thought was capable of being correct. I was also having a really hard time accepting that I was lost in an area I didn't know or recognize. I had to admit to myself that, if I was thinking at all and not just reacting, I wasn't thinking very well.

A half-hour latter, River brought me out of my mood of gloom and doom with a soft, low growl. It was the same growl he had used to warn of the thin man at our camp the night before. Now he was crouched low and showing his teeth.

"Good job, River!" I said softly, "I'll bet you've found our guy." We were climbing up a low hill and could not see what lay behind the crest of the hill about 50 yards ahead - but something would certainly be there. I quickly loaded the pistol before River and I crawled forward to the top of the hill.

Coming up the other side of the hill, more than a dozen men were walking deliberately through the trees toward us. They were mostly in a line spanning 30 or 40 yards across the forest. There were no women among them and all were dressed in green coveralls similar to those worn by the thin man we had seen the night before. Most carried a wooden stick, but now it could clearly be seen that one end was sharpened into a spear. Only one man, in the middle of the line, elderly and wearing a hat, did not carry a spear. As I watched the group walk forward in silence, it was notable that there was no metal evident in their clothing or their weapons, and the green overalls looked shinny like plastic. Even as the realization came to me that River and I were completely out-numbered by this group, I found myself wondering if this was a modern day primitive tribe or a group out of some long lost past. But this moment really didn't seem like the right time for an extraneous discussion with myself on non-essential matters; in a very short time the group would be within spear-throwing distance of my location. Since I had no idea what their intentions might be, if this meeting came down to River and me needing a head start in a footrace, I wanted the head start to be as large as possible. So I stood up and yelled. "Hello! My dog and I are lost. Can you help us?"

The line of men stopped moving abruptly, and all turned to look up at me. Some of the spears were slowly raised into a throwing position. Immediately, the man with the hat began to give orders in a language I didn't understand or recognize. No one moved or even seemed excited or surprised, and then just as slowly all the spears came down. The older man with the hat came forward two steps and with a slight British accent called out, "Well, there you are, and by Jove, you speak English! Excellent. My name is Rimu and welcome to Tenaru. You have nothing to fear from us. Kindly put away your weapon, I assure you that you will not be needing it here."

Only upon his mention of the weapon did I realize that not only was I pointing it at him, I had even taken the safety latch off. I switched the safety back to 'on' and lowered the barrel toward the ground, but did not put it away.

"I'm Al Hart", I said, "and this is my dog, River. I think we have gotten lost and we'd appreciate any help you can give us to figure out where we are. We don't intend you any harm."

The man who called himself Rimu continued to walk toward us showing a broad smile, but the others stayed where they were. Near the crest of the hill he stopped again to speak, but his gaze was fixed on River, not me. In a voice that was barely audible, seemingly talking to himself, he said, "Good heavens, a dog and a sidearm. What have I wrought?" His gaze came to me, and pointing to River, he asked calmly, "Can you control the animal?"

"Yes, but he obeys only me", I only partially lied.

"And your firearm, does it actually work?" asked Rimu. But before I could answer, Rimu's thoughts had moved on. "I think we can help you, in fact, I think we are obliged to help you. But we have come to help move your belonging to our village. My friend Rano, there, just second from the left, says you have quite a lot of stuff at your location. So we have all come to help move you. We should talk as we are walking; there are reasons why we have no time to waste."

Rimu signaled his men to follow as he started walking. The first to come forward was the man who was second from the left end of the line of men. Rano was clearly the running thin man from last evening that we were tracking. He looked trim and very strong, but not young. Obviously, he had been leading the group back toward our camp. Although no one seemed aggressive or intimidating, I was wary and concerned about the number of "them" (more than 12), verses the number of "us" (two, if you count River). Still, Rimu had offered help, and I was willing to see where this might lead.

As Rimu continued on in the direction of our camp, I spoke to River to stay close to me, and retrieved the backpack I had slipped off when River first made us aware of the presence of the men. I put the pistol in the holster on my belt, but did not close the flap over it, then slipped on the backpack. River was every bit as alert as I was, probably more so. The sight of the backpack caused Rimu to stop in his tracks. A wide smile spread across his face and excitement filled his voice.

"Have you brought the orb with you this morning?" he asked.

I felt sure he was asking about the sphere I had found in Marble Creek, but how the hell did he know about it? I was both scared and interested now, and I needed to know what he knew about the sphere and the white light. Without saying anything, I slipped off the backpack and drew the sphere from a zipped pocket. I held it chest-high in my left hand so that my right hand was free to use the gun. "Is this what you mean?" I asked.

But before I finished the sentence, the sphere was gone!

The smile never left Rimu's face, he had not spoken a word, nor had he moved an inch, but the sphere was in his hand and he appeared to be looking somewhere deep within its interior.

A couple of profanities slipped out as I thought, "Great, this SOB is some kind of magician." I called River to attention with an "at the ready" command and pulled out the pistol. With it aimed squarely between his eyes, I said "Rimu, or whoever you are, I don't know how you did that, but you are just about to find out if this gun works."

Rimu looked up from the sphere to the pistol, "I say... please. Please let me explain. You are only returning something that I have the duty of protecting. I will try to help you, but I must have the orb to do so. You may carry it if you insist; I didn't mean to upset you. But do you know what this is? Do you know how to use it? Haven't you figured out that it brought you here?" A moment later he added, "And we don't have time for a quarrel now, the green line will return before sundown and only with the orb can I hope to keep all in balance. Besides, I must be getting back. Please let us continue on our way." Without waiting for my reply, he said something to his men, turned, and walked on with his men following.

I released River from the "at the ready" command and

we followed the group, with me in a pretty foul mood. Rimu was entirely correct; I didn't know anything about the damn sphere or orb, or whatever it was. Some minutes later, I caught up with Rimu as we walked and asked why he was concerned about the green line and what it was. His good humor had returned and he was quite willing to chat.

"The green line would have found you last night. Assuming that it did find you, now there will be an inconsistent count of the people on Tenaru and it will return today to verify its count. Now that the orb has returned, I hope to use it to conceal you from the green line if I can determine how to make the request, or else hide you in a cave until it passes. We should be at your camp soon and I would ask you to show me where the green line crossed you. Based on where you were, I will try to devise a plan to recreate a consistent number."

"What if the line didn't touch us?" I asked, as I started to prioritize a hundred questions I wanted to ask him.

Rimu responded in a matter-of-fact tone, "That would have made things more easy, but that seems quite impossible."

"Listen, I'm confused as hell with what is going on, and not a lot of what you are saying makes much sense", I stammered, "but I think we were able to hide from the green line. In any case," I continued, "I don't think it touched either River or me."

"Explain to me how that would be possible", Rimu questioned gently.

"OK, we were under my boat – you'll see it when we

get to camp", I said. "If the line had penetrated the boat, we would have seen it on the ground as it passed over us, but it wasn't there, it just didn't happen. My guess is that the boat blocked the line from touching us."

There was a twinkle in Rimu's eye and he said, "I say, I've seldom found luck to be on my side since I came to Tenaru, but if your story is true, then I am keen to see this boat of yours."

After two hours of quick walking, we arrived at the camp. Rimu barely looked around before asked one of the men for his spear and used it to thump the boat. "My God", he said in amazement, "it's metal."

I told him that the boat was aluminum covered with a marine paint that I thought contained lead.

"There is no metal at all on our side of the island", Rimu explained. "This is the first metal I have ever seen here. We must move it to the village and hide it." He spoke, and two men picked up the boat and started off somewhere with it. "I'm sorry", said Rimu, "you probably don't understand. Our local dialect here is Mardu. Only two of us here speak English, my daughter and me – and I fear she is dying."

I was about to ask what he meant by "our side of the island", but the mention of his daughter dying brought on an extended quiet. I broke the silence by asking if he could tell me what was the cause of her problem.

Rimu's voice was quiet and filled with pain. "She went to a restricted route across the mountains that we call the Forbidden Pass and came back with a cut on her leg. She has become almost too hot to touch and red lines have grown up her leg from the cut. Now she can no longer speak and breathes in a beastly rapid and shallow way. I have feared the green line would return today and that we would need to get you to the village quickly, but really it is on her account that I am anxious to return home before I lose her forever. She is all the family I have left."

"Sounds like she has a bacterial infection that didn't respond to antibiotics?" I said softly, knowing I had some antibiotics in my first aid kit, but wondering if there were resistant forms of bacteria here that made useless whatever type of antibiotic Rimu might have tried to use.

"What are antibiotics?" was Rimu's answer.

Maybe he just hadn't known the English word, so I explained, "Antibiotics are a type of medicine that fights the cause of some illnesses. I don't know what is making your daughter sick, but if you think she is dying, then there is nothing to lose by trying antibiotics, if you haven't already. If you haven't tried them, I have this type of medicine with me. But we may not have much time. Let your men bring the gear; you and I can take the medicine to your daughter immediately and they can follow."

The words were barely out of my mouth when the old proverb, "never get separated from your gear" came crashing into my head. Christ, I was offering to let these guys take my stuff to where-the-hell-ever, and I'd just go off with some old magician that I didn't know from the man in the moon. No more beer and cereal for breakfast for me, ever.

Rimu looked very old at that moment, but stood arrow straight and said, "What has happened to my daughter has happened to others before – and none have lived. I am resolved to what must happen but, as her Father, I cannot abandon hope for her. If you offer her even the smallest bit of hope, I will take the risk at any cost to me. But we do not know you, or why you are here, and I think we have reason to fear you and your weapons. Our village is small and our defenses weak. If you have come to kill us, you may succeed, but I will fight you with all the power I can muster. If you have not come for that reason, then we will have much to talk about. Four men will come with us to watch you; the rest will bring your belongings. You must let me enter the village before you to prepare the people. None have seen an animal like yours that has been domesticated. Good God, none has ever seen a dog at all". After a short pause, he added; "You may see my daughter and we will try your medicine, but I shall do whatever must be done to her, or give her anything that must be given to her. Do you agree to this?"

I realized that despite his earlier smiles, Rimu was as scared and wary of me as I was of him. "Agreed" I said. "Let me get my first aid kit from the tent and I'll follow you."

For an aging man, Rimu was a strong old goat. He set our pace at a jog and maintained it for over two full hours, then rested for a brief period, and ran two more hours. We walked the last fifteen minutes because he said he didn't want to surprise any of his people. I was happy to follow his lead at that point and walk, however, I knew that River would have warned me if we were coming upon other people. Still, we had talked very little as we ran and walking allowed me enough breath to ask questions. River, Rimu, and his four men seemed un-effected by the long run. But me, I vowed to take up running again as a sport until I could do a half marathon without wheezing.

Rimu stopped on a lightly wooded hillside and pointed down to a meadow at the base of a cliff. In the trees on one side of the clearing were huts, with apparently grass-covered roofs. From the cliff, a waterfall dropped maybe 80 feet into a pool and the water spilled from the pool in a stream the size of Marble Creek, bisecting the meadow. Each side of the stream looked as if the fields had previously been planted with crops of some sort.

"Wait here until I come for you." Rimu's words were more like a command than a request. The four men also stayed to keep River and I company, or for whatever purpose Rimu had instructed.

While we waited, I wondered what antibiotics I even had to try. I figured since I really didn't know what I was doing, I better start with a broad spectrum antibiotic that could be given in big doses, as few times as possible. I had CIPRO left over from a long hike in Nepal, probably twenty tablets, but they were old. Christ, I had no idea what the shelf life of those pills might be. They were basically the size of horse pills but could be administered just twice a day. If the red lines were septicemia, then the infection was probably bacterial and CIPRO might be a good choice. If the problem was something else and the antibiotics didn't do any good, the daughter and I might both die in pretty quick succession if I got blamed for not curing her. I guess I'd never been too good at knowing when to keep my mouth shut.

Rimu returned in about 40 minutes. He had spoken to whomever he needed to and seen his daughter – from the little he said, she was doing badly. Rimu led our party into the village, followed by two of his men, River and I came next, and then two more of his men. It was clear that the priority was protecting the village from me, not the other way around. As we neared the huts, the party stopped and Rimu spoke to me directly.

"You will need to be blindfolded for the next few minutes. It is a precaution only and it will be removed quite soon."

I decided that as long as they didn't blindfold River I would probably be all right, and River would certainly be able to find this place if it ever became necessary. I allowed the blindfold to be put on my eyes and for two of the men to assist me as we walked another few minutes. When the blindfold was removed, it was clear we were in a cave. While the villagers lived in thatched huts, Rimu apparently lived in a cave. The room I saw was not large or damp, but quickly got darker as one walked toward the back of the room. In this room was a simple bed, a small table, and no other furnishings; Rimu's daughter lay there, either asleep or dead.

"How long has she been sick?" I wondered if I was too late to be of any help, regardless.

"This is the fourth day since she returned." With that statement, Rimu held up a torch and it directed a beam of light over the legs of the girl. The left leg was swollen around the ankle and there was a weeping scab covering a cut at the base of the calf. From the cut area, three red lines streaked up the leg more than twelve inches. The streaks looked a lot like septicemia, an infection where the microbes causing the problems get into the blood stream. If my guess was correct, maybe I could help; or alternatively, it could be too late already and the infection was racing toward the heart. This girl's condition might easily have been cured even a few days before, now it was going to be nip and tuck if she would make it.

I took a CIPRO from the first aid kit and explained to Rimu that he would have to crush the pill, dissolve it in the least amount of water possible and that his daughter must drink all of the mixture right now.

Although remarkably strong all day, Rimu now look tired and exhausted. "I will do as you suggest", he replied weakly. He sent two men for water and a crushing tool. While we waited, I looked over the woman without touching her. She was about 35, maybe older. Her face was thin and flushed, with eyes that were deep set and vacant. In her current state, I couldn't tell if she would be considered pretty or not. As Rimu crushed the antibiotic to dissolve it, I checked out the swollen leg again. It was ugly by any description. I wondered how the cut had become infected, and what was the bacterial organism? I was looking at the scabbed, but still oozing, cut on her leg thinking about whether it could be made to scar less if it were stitched closed. But, if she didn't live, sewing her up might be a waste of time. I heard Rimu pour water and wanted to make sure that he didn't dilute the CIPRO too much, since it was going to be hard for the patient to drink even a small amount. But as I began to look away from the wound, I noticed two very small circular punctures just below the cut. I remember thinking, "That looks like a bite mark", but my attention was now drawn to the process of dissolving the antibiotic.

Rimu sat behind his daughter and held her up as the dissolved CIPRO was given to the woman. I gave instructions to give her as much water as she could drink after she took the pill, since she had probably become dehydrated from the fever and sweating. I then suggested that each morning and evening the whole procedure was to be repeated and I left several more CIPRO tablets with Rimu. Now it was a race against time. Either the bacteria would win and she would die, or the antibiotic would win and the bacteria would be killed. One way or the other, we would have the answer in just a few days at most. I had a feeling that I had a vested personal interest in her getting better as it was possible that our lives or death were now linked.

I was again blindfolded and River and I were led to a thatched hut in the village. Our gear had arrived and been left in or around a hut, but the boat had been deliberately placed inside. Four guards had also been left outside the hut. Once my blindfold was removed, River and I sorted our stuff and found nothing missing. The hut was clean and dry, and had one grass bed on which I put my sleeping bag. I could smell fires burning outside and the odors of cooking. There seems no reason to tempt fate by testing the guards, so River and I spent the night in the hut, eating our own rations.

Morning came with no call or visit by Rimu. I was shown the latrine area by our guards, who now seemed more like "watchers" than guards. They did not try to restrain us or block our movements, but didn't seem to want us to get lost or wander off. In fact, they seemed to be very slow mentally, or perhaps they just didn't give a damn about outsiders, unlike Rimu. But then I could actually communicate with him as opposed to the crude sign language and pantomimes I tried with the guards.

River and I wandered around the hut we were assigned. I re-constructed the lean-to we had previously made out of the boat (inside the hut) and only then realized that we had not been visited the prior day by the green line. I made a mental note to ask Rimu about that. We then walked to the stream and filled our water bottles. Not knowing if the water was potable, I added two iodine tablets to each liter bottle and let twenty minutes pass before adding neutralizer tablets. This was something else to ask about, could we drink this water untreated? I had less than 100 water-treatment tablets and now wished I had brought a pump water filter instead.

The day passed and River and I were left alone to our own devices. We surveyed what we had used and what we had left from our supplies. If things went badly with Rimu's daughter, we might either not need any more supplies at all since we would also be dead, or we might need to leave in a hurry and should plan to be ready to take just what we could carry. If things went well for the woman, perhaps we could pack out to civilization with blessings (and directions) from Rimu. Toward sundown, we were brought a little food. It was entirely vegetarian and I guessed it was what had been growing in the fields by the stream. Despite the fact that it looked decidedly not fresh, I tried a little, and River was happy with his dried dog chow.

Three mornings later we woke to find Rimu at the door of our hut. His eyes looked tired but happy.

"Thank you! Thank you, she is better", he blurted out. "Your medicine is stronger than anything I have ever been able to use on Tenaru. You have brought life back to my daughter and therefore to me. Will she need more of this medicine? The change in her is remarkable; last night she sat up and spoke and this morning is drinking and eating. The heat in her is going down. I have not left her side for three days, but she is now much better." His exhausted smile told us our trial was also over and we were safe for now.

"Rimu, that is excellent news" I said, and meant it. "I'm happy I had something that would help make her better; I'm delighted for both you and your daughter. Yes, keep giving her the medicine twice a day for several more days." While I was saying these words to Rimu, I was thinking to myself, "Damn, the Gods of Luck are smiling on you, Al. Sometimes even a blind squirrel finds an acorn, and, boy, you got lucky today." I gave Rimu five more days worth of CIPRO pills, leaving me with, I think, eight remaining. When he left, the guards, or watchers, went with him.

Now River and I appeared to be unwatched and free to roam around. Each morning and evening we were brought a small amount of food and we were left undisturbed. I felt all dressed up with no place to go. There was food and water here in the village, but I had no more idea where I was than when we realized that we had lost Marble Creek following the night of the white light. To make matters worse, I had lost the sphere to Rimu, and he had hinted that it had been involved in bringing us "here", wherever here is. Disturbing memories of Rimu's phrases like "no metal on our side of the island" kept coming back to me. What island? There are no islands by Marble Creek. It seemed like I would need Rimu and his people if I hoped to learn where we were or how to get back home.

# Chapter 3

## Night in the Alzheimer's ward

*This part I know to be real. I remember writing these words and the miserable situation of being in some sort of hospital or old folks home.*

Even in the dark I can recognize that I'm in my room on some sort of ward; there is a distinctive yellow glow from one of the medical monitors, a wall clock with luminescent hands that now reads 2:56am, and light from the night-light in the bathroom (that is never shut off) spilling out into the bedroom. I woke up tonight feeling excited and agitated, but don't know why. As if anything exciting ever happened in this place. I remember the doctors talking about me having had a possible stroke, but I don't remember having any problem. Still, here I am and I can't move. I think I'm screaming, but no one can hear. It takes forever for me to move my eyes from one place to another, and no one has the patience to notice. And since I can't communicate with anyone, I have to remember all my thoughts until morning when I'm placed at a table with a computer and can write them down. All day yesterday my mind was clear and I spent the day considering my situation and writing this down. Apparently that doesn't happen very often since my computer shows few examples of discussions with myself of my current situation, but lengthy stories of unknown authorship, that mean nothing at all to me, but tell of adventures I am having with my dog, River.

How did I get like this? What could have pushed me

to such a state?  Was it a fluke of genetics that something physical broke down and left me incapacitated, or just an escape mechanism from trying to deal with everyone else's problems as well as my own?  I'd often thought of "getting away from it all" with respect to work, leaving the university to be a hermit, but couldn't do it due to a sense of need to be able to help my son and possibly even help others (mostly students) at the school.  But I never imagined such a horrible consequence of "getting away from it all" as I am now living.  I would have thought that if I were to have a physical problem it would have shown up when I exercised every morning – there were days when I really pushed myself through tough workouts.  It's easier for me to think that my condition resulted somehow from trying to do a job (university administration) that has made me more than half crazy over the last ten years.  I liked most of the people, but couldn't stand the thoughtless decisions and the pretense that poor choices weren't being made on a regular basis.  For years I rationalized the actions of bosses for whom the university was all about them personally, not about the institution or the students.  For years I put up with faculty colleagues who thought the world revolved around them, and the purpose of the university was to protect them from students.  For decades I watched as retention and graduation rates dropped and departments taught what they wanted, but not what the students needed.  Just last night, as I lie awake, I relived the memory of a research trip to Cuba I took years ago.  No wonder I'm a basket case now.  And the funny part is that the Cuban trip was actually a rather fun and successful trip; but it got me started thinking of the people and events that might have (certainly should have) driven me over the mental cliff and into this sorry state of life – if one wants to call this living.

Let me use some examples. I've got nothing now but time to write, and I've compiled a mental list of stories from work at Utopia University, all true, although some seem unbelievable even to me. Perhaps it makes sense to start with our University's Provost and how I became the Dean and follow that saga with the story of a recent trip to Cuba. I'm hoping to present a taste of my life the last ten years and illustrate some examples of our administration and faculty. Maybe that, along with a few other truly strange stories, will set the stage for understanding what I had and what I have lost.

Utopia University (UU) sits in an envious location; it's adjacent to a large lake and just a few miles from a mountain range, convenient for water sports, biking and snowboarding. Spokane, WA, is not too far away, and the sophisticated student or faculty member can take a bus there directly from the town where campus is located. Canada, where the drinking age is 18, is just a few hours drive further for the less sophisticated student. The fraternity and sorority parties are closer still. The campus sports teams excel at doing badly so there is ample opportunity for student riots, the University President resides on campus so there is adequate opportunity for students to express displeasure, and there is an active faculty union that pickets each time the contract negotiations don't go as they wish. The union routinely sends articles and paid ads to the local newspapers telling parents not to send their children to UU, as the school is unfair to its faculty. That last point is interesting since the tuition paid by the students also pays the salaries of the faculty members; but academic freedom allows them to act against their own economic interest in good conscience. No one has been denied tenure, for any reason, for the last

15 or more years and now those who should not have been tenured are the gatekeepers for those going up for tenure. But UU religiously guards it secrets as part of its traditions, since negative stories are considered negative for student recruitment, and UU counts student numbers in terms of dollars of revenue.

So, why do students pay to go to UU? There are only four main questions students ask to help determine if they will go to any school. Is it expensive? (No, in the case of UU). Is it recognized for excellence? (No, for UU). Is it easy to get in? (Yes, for UU). And, is the location great for "extra curricular" events? (Yes, for UU). So students come, unaware that they will get more than they bargained for in the form of interesting characters and stories, and less in education. Still, where else but in higher education do people say, "Take my money and give me the least I can get for this!" And so they come to UU; and are sometimes surprised by what they find.

*The Provost*

Chris, the Provost and Vice President for Academic Affairs at UU, had never been in charge of an academic unit or college, or served as Chair of a Department, before becoming second in command at the university. He had gone from being the Director of the Equal Opportunity Office to being Provost, when the President appointed him without a search. During his years in the position of Provost, Chris's claim to fame at UU was how clearly he demonstrated the validity of the Peter Principle.

At that point in history, Dr. Al Hart (me) was a fledgling administrator and Full Professor, answering to a Dean, who, in turn, answered to the Provost. For the previous four years I had served as an Associate Dean in the College of Life Sciences and Agriculture. A year after I was hired as Assoc. Dean, the Dean who hired me stepped down and a new Dean (Martin) was brought in from outside of UU. For the last three years, several of us had watched in horror as the department chairs (that made up the college Executive Council) and Martin, the Dean at that time, had fought for control of the direction of the college. The dean, charged by the Provost to re-organize the college and increase efficiencies, sought to direct the chairs to improve faculty workloads and modernize the curriculum. The chairs, as advocates for the status quo, used a combination of collective bargaining agreement issues, college by-laws, and "shared governance" principles to maintain the comfortable positions of no responsibility into which they had molded themselves over decades. After nearly three years of fighting, the Dean's figurative 'pry-bar' had proven not long enough to get the necessary leverage to move the department chairs, the increases in efficiency were too slow in coming, and the college had generated a projected financial deficit well in excess of a million dollars for the year just ending (with a growing accumulated deficit that was starting to rival the national debt). The college situation was looking pretty ugly at best.

Unfortunately, no help for any Dean was to be forthcoming from Chris the Provost. The two Associate Deans of our college had always considered Martin's requests to Central Administration, via the Provost, about as beneficial as asking Bonnie and Clyde to help the Wells-Fargo Bank manage its cash. Chris was widely considered akin to an oily politician whose job was to keep his job. Requests for new teaching faculty had resulted in the Provost initiating a hiring freeze until the financial deficits of the College of Life Sciences and Agriculture were eliminated. Chris also had a vacation villa on the Isle of Crete and was known to host the university President at his villa any time a "scam" could be worked to have the university send them to Europe; Chris's favor with the President was assumed to be very high.

One Friday afternoon, while the then-Dean, Martin, was on a trip to speak at a conference in Alaska and I had been left to manage the day-to-day operations of the college, I received a phone call from the Dean. Martin was still in Alaska but wanted to talk even prior to returning to UU. It seems that after a scheduled phone meeting with the Provost, in which the first 40 minutes were taken up by routine work-related discussions, there was an "Oh, by the way" moment just before the call ended. The Provost informed Dean Martin that he would be asked to step down from his position at the end of the academic year, some four months hence. Martin informed the Provost that he would indeed step down, if Chris was determined to remove him, but would leave the position in two weeks. The Dean had called to let me know the situation.

"Al, you'll need to know that I'm stepping down – not by choice – and that I've recommended to the Provost that you become the interim dean. You will almost certainly be hearing from Chris soon, so be thinking about what you are going to want if you take the job. But I'd suggest that you not trust that SOB very far", Martin advised.

I left work for home shortly thereafter, mildly in shock, and hoping to have the weekend to think about what was happening. Did I want the job? What would I ask for if I took the position? Was the college in a position to be saved or would I just be expected to manage the decline?

The prospect of simply managing decline was not appealing regardless of the promises that might come with the position of interim Dean. It would be one of those long weekends of endless possibilities, but of little sleep. One nagging, recurrent realization centered on my recognition that the Dean that was stepping down was extremely smart, very experienced, and remarkably knowledgeable. Martin was not a "warm and fuzzy" personality, but was very competent. The current Dean's problem(s) as an administrator seemed to reside in his ability to out-think the Provost and a willingness to occasionally cross swords with Chris on issues that actually mattered. Each time hope glimmered in my mind that I could indeed manage the college and I saw opportunity and promise to change the culture of the college, the recurrent realization of the competence of the current dean would sneak into my thoughts and suck the wind out of my sails, leaving me to questions if it was management skills that were needed or an ability to suck up to the Provost.

Late in the night (or early in the morning), after perhaps a few drinks, I felt I had distilled the problem to its essence. First, I didn't know anything about the college budget; that had been the domain of the Dean. Second, I did know that I would be in the same position as Martin in trying to direct the Department Chairs and the Executive Council. The two problems were linked at the hip, if one couldn't control the deficit, one could not be successful as the Dean. If one couldn't work with the Executive Council, one couldn't change the culture of the departments or control the finances. In a moment of weakness, I made up my mind; I would accept the position as the new Dean with the following conditions:

1. I would ask to be appointed as the Dean, not as an interim.
2. I would need the Provost's permission to replace all of the departmental Chairs that made up the college Executive Council. The departments would be asked to elect new Chairs, but I would want veto power over any names submitted by the departments.

A new start was needed, and with these changes, I felt I would be willing to take up the mantle of the Dean.

On Monday, the expected call from the Provost was received. I was not comforted when Chris asked me to meet with him but he was not willing to reveal the purpose of the meeting. I would need to remember to thank Martin for the kindness of his "heads up" phone call.

The meeting went better than I had expected. The Provost announced that the old dean was stepping down and I was being considered as the interim replacement. In order to insure continuity, the decision of a successor would be made as quickly as possible. Chris spoke, "Do you have any thoughts on whether you would be interested, or what you might need to accept this offer?" I let my requirements just slip out one at a time in a manner that did not suggest that I had prepared in advance.

I said, "I will need the authority to make decisions and changes and, therefore, I would need to carry the title of the dean, not as an interim, but as the Dean.

"OK, I'll have to think about that", said the Provost.

" I'd like to replace all the Chairs and Directors and reconstitute the college Executive Committee", I said as evenly as I could.

"Jesus Christ!" the Provost explained, "that's serious business. Can't you make the existing team work?"

"No".

"Alright, I'll think about it and get back to you. Your term, if we can agree, will be for three, not five, years and the salary will be $10K less than the current salary of the old dean. Anything else?" The Provost's tone indicated the discussion was over.

I left feeling pretty good. In less than 15 minutes, I had asked for everything of importance I wanted and the ball was firmly in the Provost's court now. It was pretty sure there would be no further negotiations, just a "yes" or "no" at this point. I was a little miffed that I would be expected to do everything the old dean had been doing, and expected to fix the problems as well, but would not even receive the same salary. Oh well, the offer was still a raise for me and good old Chris had to get his pound of flesh. Assuming that all went well, once the paperwork was done, I would start implementing my plans.

Two days later Chris called to say he had drafted the paperwork for my appointment as the dean and the position would not be interim. Indeed, it seemed all of my conditions would be met. But when I picked up the agreement, I was surprised to find that no mention was made of the request to change all the department Chairs and reconstitute the Executive Committee. No need, I was told, since this was not a contractual point, but an agreement between a dean and the provost. It did not need to be in writing, but was acceptable to the provost and I could start as dean immediately on signing the appointment letter. That wasn't entirely correct since Martin still had a number of work-days left before he had agreed to step down; yet after finally landing in the dean's position some days later, I had almost a week of new job "honeymoon".

It was time to implement the plans that I (now dean Hart) had formulated during that long weekend some weeks before. I added a discussion of the chairs positions to the Executive Committee agenda. Perhaps there really was hope for college and the sun would shine in our back door someday…

When my meeting with the Department Chairs came, I explained my negotiated conditions for accepting the dean's position and announced the plan to reconstruct the Executive Committee. I explained that I was requesting each current member's resignation and that each department should now vote and send a name the department wanted to serve as the next Department Chair to the dean's administrative assistant. The dean (me) would reserve the right to veto any name. I would, I told them, come by each current chair's office individually to personally tell them if I would accept the re-nomination of each current chair, in order to prevent them the embarrassment of having their name forwarded but subsequently vetoed. Thinking about those one-on-one meetings at a later time, I can suggest they were among the least pleasant memories I can recall, including when, as a young man, the chain on my bike had slipped at full speed, causing both my feet to slide off the peddles and landing me, testicles first, on the bar of my bike. That landing on the bar, worse than the resulting bike wreck, was nothing compared to the individual meetings with the chairs. I was off to a roaring start as the dean.

I thought the worst was over, following my meetings

with the Chairs, as I trudged up to the Administration building for a bi-weekly meeting with the Provost. However, I quickly realized that I was mistaken when, while I was waiting my turn to meet with the Provost, I saw all nine of the Department Chairs from my College leave the Provost's office as a group. I instantly guessed that the Provost had been placed in the position of deciding whether he would make nine Chairs happy and one Dean unhappy, or vice versa. It was a no-brainer for him. Momentarily I was to learn that the Provost had changed his mind about our agreement and that I was not to change the Executive Committee of the College. There was a sinking feeling in my stomach as I realized that my plans for the College no longer had a chance of being realized. In a figurative manner, I had poured gasoline on the Executive Committee and lit them on fire. Now, I was being told to hose them off and work with them. If working relations had been bad before, it was really going to be interesting going forward.

I walked back to my office and took down the sign that said "Welcome Dean Hart". I'd have left it up if it had said, "Welcome Dean Hart, how does it feel to be a Eunuch?" Or even if it had said, "Welcome to the road to crazy."

*The Faculty*

The faculty members at UU ranged from the great to the not so great. It was all a matter of one's perspective. Some were excellent researchers, but lousy teachers, others the reverse. Each was a smart, independent individual; each was looking out for himself, or herself. Each had aspects for which they were famous and aspects that should have gotten them fired.

Dr. Bruce Horton was famous for his office. Faculty and students walked out of their way to pass by Bruce's office in hopes of finding the door open. Two walls were lined with bookshelves that were completely filled with books. It appeared that not even a credit card could be slid into any of the shelves. But the main draw for the curious was the floor-to-ceiling piles of books and boxes not on any shelf, and the desk that held so many piles of loose papers that no one had seen the desk top in years. There was a Y-shaped path through the books and collected "stuff" leading to the desk. A single channel from the door to the edge of the desk then branched to a single chair in front of the desk and around to a chair behind the desk for Dr. Horton. He was truly an example of the absent-minded professor. For instance, he never started a conversation because he could never remember who were his students and who were faculty members. It was said that Bruce had never bought a book, but that the horded collection was from booksellers who would provide a free "examination copy" of a text or book, to be reviewed and either used in a class or returned. However, none were ever returned by Dr. Horton, and if Bruce couldn't find a book he wanted, even if he owned it, he would order the same one again. His papers and exams were filed by turning one group sideways to the group below it. As the piles grew, the precise angles were lost and the piles began to resemble circular towers of paper several feet high. Heavy weights on top kept the piles from toppling due to air currents or brushes from Bruce's coat. Some student had taped a "Bio-Hazard" sign on one paper pile on the side of the desk that Bruce couldn't see, but it was clearly visible to anyone sitting in the student's chair. The middle of the desk was limited to piles of paper not higher than 12 inches since Bruce needed to see over them to view any student in the single chair on the other side of the desk. All other space in the office was filled with books, piles of papers, or boxes of unknown artifacts. It was speculated that an equivalent of half of the California redwood forests had been killed to provide the paper filling Bruce's office.

Dr. Horton was in his late 40s or early 50s and was a quiet man known for his acquired knowledge rather than his ability to pass it on to students. His area of study was the decline of rural farming and his interests were in sustainable agriculture. He was married, had no kids, and seemed never to socialize, with only the exception of college or departmental events at which he felt obligated to make an appearance. He usually drank very sparingly and was considered quite gentlemanly and polite. He had a respectable beer belly and a remarkable comb-over hairstyle, very short on one side of the line where he parted his remaining hairs, but very long on the other side, with the long hairs combed completely across his shiny dome to cover much of his rapidly balding head. Still, his peers always looked to see if he was present at parties since there were rumors that, when he was in situations where he was not know by anyone, he became a true party animal - and all hoped they would be present should such a display occur. The Provost at UU, had made it very clear to all senior administrators that any "excitement" involving Dr. Horton was to be maintained in strict confidence as not to embarrass the university.

Only three people (four if you count Dr. Horton) knew of the last such occurrence of Dr. Horton's unique response to alcohol: Dr. Tom Martin, Tom's student (a Ph.D. candidate) named Judy Taylor, and me. Tom had learned of an opportunity to visit Cuba to do research on sustainable agriculture. Cuba had become a living laboratory for this topic area since the loss of Russian support. No gasoline existed there to run the tractors, so animal traction (oxen) was being used widely to plow fields. No pesticides were available, so bio-control was used on a large scale to control pests. No fertilizer was being imported, so everything that hit the ground was being composted. UU had started some sustainability initiatives, including a sustainability office run by Tom Martin. Tom and his graduate student, Judy, had asked Bruce Horton and me of our interest in joining them on this trip. This would be right up Bruce's academic area, and it was considered that including me, as the Dean of Agriculture, would give our delegation more clout as seen by the Cuban officials deciding on whom to give visas. As for me, I'd never been to Cuba, and I decided I could use the excuse that I was needed to keep an eye on Dr. Bruce Horton.

With official research license papers in hand, we flew to Mexico and from there to Cuba. After just over a week of productive meetings and agricultural visits, we found ourselves back in Havana waiting to see if the hurricane *de jour* would chase us out of the country. We expected to be leaving on several hours notice anytime in the next thirty-six hours, whenever there was room on a departing plane. So, at the end of a day spent waiting to hear if there was room for us to board a plane, we decided to take in some Cuban music and 'the sights' out on the edge of Havana, hoping the rain would hold off until after we had left. As the evening progressed, Bruce went from not drinking, to sipping excellent quality rum, to a rum-mint drink favored by many in the jazz clubs. Bruce exhibited a real liking for his Mojitos and soon began to drink them with gusto, like water. He was singing loudly, but not in tune, as we left the club. The rest of us agreed a walk might help Bruce sober up, so we walked along the dark street by some old tourist clubs. Outside of one of these clubs, sitting in a chair, was an old man selling baby chickens. Judy wanted to hold a chick and, as she got one from the box, Tom, the only one of us who know Spanish well, asked the old man why he was sitting there at night selling chicken. The old man pointed over to a small fenced area and said in broken English, "The chickens for him." Looking in the enclosure, we saw a sleeping alligator. The baby chicks were being sold to feed to the alligator.

Bruce seemed instantly to sober up, and came alive with a vigor none had ever seen in him. He paid for a baby chicken and rushed over to pen. With care, he tossed the chick within a foot of the alligator's head. But the alligator, it just lay there.

Bruce screamed! "That's my chicken, bite its head off". But the alligator, it just lay there. "Get my chicken! Bite its fucking head off." The alligator apparently couldn't be bothered.

In the mean time, Tom had asked the old man, in Spanish, if it had been a busy day for him. The man replied it had, since the storm was coming, the Gringo's had spent their money and were leaving. This day he had sold many baby chickens; it had been a good day. The alligator, it seems, wasn't hungry anymore.

But Bruce was obsessed. His cries became shrill, "That's my chicken, bite its fucking head off". "You stupid alligator, don't you know what to do? Bite its fucking head off. That's MY chicken, bite it's fucking head off."

A heavy rain began to fall, but still the alligator

remained as immobile as a rock. I began to worry about what the Provost had meant by "excitement involving Bruce" and wondered if he knew more than he had shared with me.

To add salt to Bruce's wound, the baby chicken walked over to the alligator and across one of its feet. The alligator just lay there. Bruce went crazy; in less than a second he had jumped over the wall into the pen and ran up to the alligator screaming, "That's my chicken, bite its fucking head off!"

Bruce's back blocked Judy's view of what was happening, and when she saw Bruce was not interested in the alligator, to her relief, she assumed that he was going to rescue the chick. Bruce had indeed picked up the baby chicken, and as he turned to leave the pen, he spit the chick's head out of his mouth. It was a scene from a nightmare movie. The wind and rain had destroyed Bruce's comb-over, and wet stringy hair hung long down the side of his face, matted with rain and blood that ran from his mouth; he was wild-eyed and oblivious to the alligator that was slowly walking off as if annoyed. Judy feinted.

It took some time to get everyone back to the hotel. Bruce spent the night talking to the porcelain God; Judy recovered more quickly, but has never since said a word to Dr. Horton, as far as anyone knows. I swore Tom and Judy to silence, with the exception of the times when the three of us have drinks at my house and relive the entire episode in howls of laughter. Bruce has never mentioned the event to any of the three of us and seems to assume that it never happened.

I spent years resisting the temptation to replace the "Bio-Hazard" sign that Bruce doesn't know is in his office with one that says "Bite its Fucking head off". I've come to realize that one can get post-traumatic stress disorder as readily from "herding cats (read faculty)" as from overseas conflicts. I think I will coin a new phrase: "post-administrative stress disorder".

# Chapter 4

## Rimu's Story: Tenaru

*This is the second part of a story I (and maybe you) am living vicariously through what I read. I suspect I wrote it, but have no knowledge or recollection of any part of this story.*

Tenaru was getting perceptibly warmer. I had left for a two-week camping trip the end of October and now been gone for about three weeks, so that put my best guess at the date about a week or so from December. But rather than needing more and warmer clothes, I was often going without a coat at all. Mornings were still cool, but the days were getting warm. Time and date were now really no more than a guess. I had set the time on my watch by what I remembered the time to be when the sun went down, and the date on the watch said Nov. 21. But something was clearly not right; the hours of daylight seemed to be getting longer, not shorter. The weather was getting warmer and nothing here seemed like it was closing in on Christmas. The only consistent fact seemed to be that the food I had brought with me was running out.

For the last two weeks, I had seen Rimu only in passing or for a few very short visits. He had suggested that much was going on for him at the moment and several times asked that I excuse his poor hospitality, but his work was very demanding just now. I assumed that he had meant presiding over his village, since on one short visit he asked if I could oversee the workers building a dike to prevent the annual flooding of one of the crop fields. He said he would let the workers know to follow my orders, but that they had instructions already on how to start. They had worked for the last two weeks at a painfully slow place, using no tools except long pry bars and baskets, to build a small dike. It slowly became clear why I had been asked to oversee a project I knew almost nothing about; the workers were mentally slow and without direction. It was obvious that the intent of the project was to prevent the spring run-off of water over the falls from flooding one of the fields on the side of the stream with the lower bank. A curve in the stream below the falls, coupled with a high bank on the far side of the stream, directed all the overflow water into a field and created a lake running up toward the huts. When this lake formed, it apparently blocked access to both Rimu's cave and to the main stream crossing site that in turn affected the use of the fields on one side of the stream until the floods stopped and the lake dried up. Thirty men had been assigned the task. They brought rocks and earth in baskets and built a six-foot high rock wall for perhaps eighty yards along the bank, then covered it with dirt. I learned from the tracks that the rocks and earth had come from Rimu's cave. The men almost never spoke. When they did, the conversation in Mardu was clipped and short, seldom more than two sentences, and I understood not a single word. The efforts of the men reminded me of what I would have expected of cavemen – following a general plan with no leadership and no care if someone else did something well or poorly.

I would learn how little they cared about everything when one day a large man carrying a basket of rocks and dirt turned his ankle on a loose rock and fell. The basket of rocks he carried crushed his arm between the basket and the rocks he was crossing, breaking the arm and leaving it at a painful-looking right angle to what it should have been. If I had not seen the man fall, I probably would not have known the accident occurred. The man made no sound but waited for help to free his broken arm and began to replace rocks in his basket with his good arm. I could see the improbable angle of his arm and ran to help. He let me look at his arm, but seemed not to care what I was doing at all. I looked at the others and yelled, "Rimu, Rimu", and pointed toward Rimu's cave. At last, one of the men got up and slowly walked off toward the cave.

Rimu came down the site of the accident only moments later. After a quick assessment of the situation, he said, "I am sure your medicine is much stronger than mine, can you re-set the arm?"

"Sure", I said, "but it is going to hurt like hell. I can give him something that will help with the pain later, but I don't have anything that will kill the pain immediately, and I'm afraid his arm will swell too much if we wait before we do this".

"No worries, mate", Rimu replied cheerfully, "he won't care". With that explanation, he spoke to several other men in Mardu and they held the large man down. "Oh, he'll fell the pain and will reflexively or instinctively try to avoid it", he said, "so we will hold him down, but he won't care about the pain at all. Please go right ahead".

"What do you mean he won't care?" I asked. "God damn it, just wait a minute and let me get ready." I turned to River, "Bring the first aid kit, GO!"

River returned in a moment with his head through the shoulder straps of the daypack that contained my first aid kit, dragging it under his head and trying not to step on the loose straps that played along the ground. I had found some sticks to support the arm, and from my first aid pack, I got out the materials to make a splint: one of two large square pieces of cloth, some ointment for the cuts and abrasions the arm had received from being crushed, a codeine-based tablet for pain, and a couple of bandages and tape.

"OK, let's do this. Are your men ready?" I asked Rimu. He nodded. I straightened the arm and reset the position of the bone. The man flinched and every muscle in his body became tight, but he made no sound; his eyes didn't close nor did they show anger or pain. I put bandages on the cuts and scrapes, put a splint on the arm and fashioned a sling from the cloth so he couldn't move the arm.

"Good on you, mate!" said Rimu to me, as he turned and headed back toward his cave. "Jolly well done", he called back.

The large man with the broken arm continued to work with one arm until we finished for the day.

I had modified the original plan for the dike and had drawn my new idea in the dirt so it would be understood. I wanted a "diversion wall" to re-direct the full force of flood waters from hitting the new dike head-on, but I also knew that the village could get double duty out of the diversion wall if we placed it correctly, so that at low water we could use it to feed an irrigation canal that they could build later. What good was working in a College of Life Sciences and Agriculture if one couldn't apply some practical knowledge?

In the weeks we worked on the dike, I had seen Rimu

only three times, including at the accident. The work on the dike had given me something to do and was a welcome chance to repay the kindness of this tribe or village. But now I was really anxious to get some time with Rimu, despite however busy he was, and to get some answers. My vacation was over a couple of weeks ago and I was AWOL from my job, I was almost out of food, even though we had gone on strict rations to conserve what we had remaining, and River and I were totally lost with no idea where we were. Worst, I couldn't talk with the village people, tribe, savages, or whatever they were. There was something wrong with these folks; they were like stone-age people or perhaps mentally impaired. I began to wonder if I had gone back in time. River and I had been treated very well, without a doubt, but we were no closer to answers about our situation than the day Rimu and his group found us. I resolved to have River lead me to Rimu's cave in the morning and ask him to sit down for a chat – and not to take no for an answer.

The next morning was bright and sunny, and promised to be warm, as River and I headed off toward Rimu's cave. I decided we would go first to the stream, as if to inspect the dike, and then follow the trail of the workers who had carried baskets from the cave to the construction site. As well as we were being treated, I didn't want the village folks to see River and me heading to the cave and wonder (if they thought at all) what we were up to. I was comfortable that I would not need the gun with Rimu or in this village so, before leaving, I hid it with some care in case we were lucky enough to be gone awhile and in case one of the mentally slow folks just wandered into our hut.

Twenty yards from the head of the dike was a bend in

the path toward the cave and if we could pass those twenty yards without attracting notice we should no longer be visible to the people of the village. As we neared the dike head, I watched for a break in the people's activity, preparing to run full speed across the space to the bend. The break came and, as I took my first step into a run, a figure appeared at the bend walking toward us. Almost tripping, I dropped to one knee and pretended to be tying my shoe. Approaching us was a beautiful young lady whom I had not seen before in the village. In fact, this was only the second woman I had seen in the whole time I'd been here. As she saw us, a big smile broke across her face.

"Hello", she said in English, "You are, of course, Dr. Hart, but I do not know what to call your animal. I am Hanish, Rimu's daughter, and my Father tells me that you saved my life - and maybe his because you saved me".

"You're Rimu's daughter?" I asked dumbfounded. "Does he have more than one?"

"No", laughed Hanish, "I am all there is, and I wanted to thank you for what you have done for me. Unfortunately for me, Dad has been so worried about me that he has only let me come outside today, although I've felt perfectly fine for at least a week".

I realized that this young lady had been so sick when I last saw her that I hadn't recognized her now that she was well. "Anyone with antibiotics would have done as well as I in curing you", I stammered, "but I'm very happy to see you are well. Oh, and by the way, please call me Al and this", I said pointing to the dog, "is River".

She gave a big smile to each of us, and Hanish continued: " My father would like to extend an invitation for you" and then she added belatedly, "and River, to share the evening meal with us in our house tomorrow. I will come to show you the way. Dad says there are things he would like for you to know and he is pretty sure there is much that you are anxious to ask. I hope you will accept; we both owe you quite a lot".

"It is our pleasure to accept your invitation, but you owe us nothing and we will hope only for your friendship", I replied, hoping not to have sounded too corny. Her invitation had seemed semi-formal and I wanted to be sure that my acceptance showed enough formality and respect not to offend anyone and get us uninvited. This was better than I had even hoped for – my plan had been to try to coerce answers from Rimu - now he was offering to freely give then to us.

Back at our hut, I was delighted with the events of the day. Tomorrow, we would have a chance for answers and now there were two English speakers to talk with – one quite beautiful and with a name other than "Rimu's daughter".

The following evening, Hanish came to collect River and me just as she had offered. There was no suggestion of a blindfold this time; we simply followed her up past the waterfall at the head of the stream, perhaps two tenths of a mile, to the entrance to a cave.

At the entrance, a small room was dimly lit with ambient light from outside. It was plain and had a dirt floor; this room had only a rough table, two chairs and two beds made of grass on the floor. I recognized this room as where I had first seen Hanish when she was so sick. But Hanish walked directly through this space to the dark, far wall of the room. Just before I lost sight of her in the darkening cave, she paused, asked us to wait a moment, and that she would be back to lead us. I heard her take several steps to the corner of the room and then the sound of something sliding on a well-greased track. Seconds later, I felt her hand on my shoulder and she asked me to take her hand so she could lead us a short distance. We went several steps along a pitch-dark "dog leg" corridor. I kept my free hand on the wall as I followed and after just a few steps it narrowed so that I had to turn sideways to continue, but shortly afterward I felt a hole or a door in the wall. Once we passed through, Hanish stopped us once more and again I heard the sound of sliding which I now assumed was the closing of the "door" we had just past through. A few steps more led us around another "dog leg" into the light.

This part of the cave was magnificent! A crack in the ceiling of the cave, ranging from two to five yards wide, rose thirty feet with almost perfectly vertical walls. The crack, allowing in the afternoon light, split the cave into a large and small room with several visible openings to other rooms or corridors. The cave was protected from the elements except directly under the open crack, and there a small stream ran in a gravel channel. This bigger room of the cave had a large cooking area, woven grass partitions were hung to separate the area into rooms, and the spaces I could see were well appointed with wooden furniture, including bed frames, dressers, storage cabinets, finished tables and chairs, and wood floors. I was amazed; the village people lived in grass huts, cooked on outdoor fires, and had the mental capacity of children. Rimu and Hanish lived in the lap of luxury by comparison. I mentally added another dozen questions to the list for which I needed answers this evening.

"Welcome", said Rimu to me, "and thank you for collecting our guests", he added to Hanish. "What do you think of our home? Hanish and I have worked on this for fifteen years now".

"It's really amazing and I'm so surprised that I don't really know what to say", I blurted out. "But if you can live like this, why do the people in the village live like primitives? Is something wrong with them? Are you their leader? Why are they so mentally slow and you are not? Did you bring me here, and where the hell is "here"? What is the…", I asked, realizing that with each question I was speaking more quickly and more loudly, until Rimu interrupted.

"Wait, wait. We will take your questions one at a time but let's start at the beginning. We will eat first and then I will tell you a story by the fire that will answer many of your questions. Anything that you still need to ask you may ask before we send you home", Rimu promised.

"Send us home?", I stammered, "Home here or where I came from? Can you send us back where we came from?"

"Yes, I think I can send you back", Rimu said softly, placing an emphasis on the word 'you', "but you will need some background first. The evening will be long enough without interruptions, so let us eat and get started. Hanish please prepare the food", he said with sufficient authority to quiet me and send his daughter into action.

After a delicious meal, but one with less than ample serving size by my standards, we moved to chairs by the fire. Rimu put his feet up to get more comfortable and Hanish covered him with a square of the same green cloth worn by each person we had seen. I sat opposite Rimu with River on the floor at my side. Hanish sat on the floor on the other side of River and stroked his fur.

After a heavy sigh, Rimu began, "Where should I start? First, I will tell you that I have given you every opportunity to harm the population of our village, even though I have had you watched every moment. Had you come here to harm us, you could have done so, yet you have not. Indeed, you have saved my daughter and helped my people and brought us no harm. Now I have come to trust you. Next, let me apologize for the meager portions of our meal. Hanish has become an excellent cook, but we have little food with which to create gourmet meals. No, let me correct that, we have little food that does not contain the compound Thimlomarium. Only the food we grow here on Tenaru during the summer does not contain Thimlomarium, and we cannot yet grow enough for everyone. You will not know of this chemical compound, Thimlomarium; the first versions of the compound, created accidently many, many years ago, reduced mental capacity, removed all sexual drive, and greatly increased one's tolerance to pain. Chinese leaders were the first to use the compound to control people and they devised several variations that improved its ability to allow the management of great numbers of people, leading to the version of Thimlomarium that now influences our lives. When Thimlomarium accumulates in human bodies, the results are what you have seen in the people of the village".

Speaking to me, Rimu continued, "You are now, while you stay here on Tenaru, accumulating small amounts of

Thimomarium in your body, mostly from contaminated fish you have caught in the river, and you must be sent somewhere to clean out your system before it accumulates in order to prevent you from suffering the symptoms of the people you have observed here on Tenaru. We have no shortage of food, just a shortage of food without Thimlomarium. Within the next four days, the green line that you hide from when you first arrived here will return. It is, among other purposes, a scanning device that counts the people on Tenaru. Had it scanned you, when you first arrived, it would have registered an incorrect number and returned the next day to conduct a re-count, which is why we came so quickly to find you so we could arrange for the re-count to be "correct". I had no idea that your metal boat could protect you from being scanned, but it did and so the count remained as it had been and no recount was necessary. However, it is almost time now for the next population count, and that is always followed by a food delivery. Unfortunately, the food that will be delivered is liberally, and deliberately, laced with Thimlomarium".

"Who would deliberately put this "thimlo" stuff in your food, who does the counting, and where does the food come from?" I interrupted.

"Patience, please", said Rimu, "I have only just started and you must let me tell the story. I hope it will answer most of your questions and help you understand your situation - as well as our situation. You have been an unexpected gift to us and I would give much to convince you to stay on Tenaru, but you must not be here when the green line returns and already it will take 24 hours in an environment without Thimlomarium to clear your body of the compound that is slowly building up. I cannot let you become like the rest of my people for that would greatly reduce your ability to help us".

"I did not intend to bring you here", Rimu continued, shifting his position, "but you somehow became involved with the orb and accompanied it when the orb returned here. That was an unexpected accident. Because I didn't expect you, or trust you when we first met, you were allowed to assume that we were a village of simpletons, which is mostly true due to the Thimlomarium that is in our food. But our situation is more sinister than that. The island of Tenaru is, in fact, a prison, and the people here are political prisoners. All of the villagers were once leaders of an opposition group that challenged the ruling power of the current Manuka party leaders. But both resistance and opposition to the Manuka party have been eliminated in the last 15 years through the use of Thimlomarium and the orbs. I was, at one time 15 years ago, the second-in-command of the Manuka party but resisted the plans of our Prime Minister to consolidate power and create a permanent ruling party, if not a dictatorship. After I faked my own death, my wife and daughter were sent here because my wife was, in her own right, a charismatic leader and therefore a political threat. How I escaped to Tenaru with the master orb is a long story for another time. The Manuka control the strongest of the three civilizations on this planet, because of treachery and because they controlled the master orb, indeed, all the orbs. But we will get to that soon enough".

"You are not now in the time you know or in the location you know, but you are still on the Earth, just not the one you knew. You have not gone back in time as the villagers might suggest, rather you have been moved 350

years into your future and to a location half way around the
world from where you originated when the orb brought
you here. If I were not a student of history, I would not be
able to tell you that Tenaru is an area that in your time was
called Stuart Island, a part of New Zealand. The
headquarters of the Manuka party is about six miles away
across the water at the south end of the South Island of
New Zealand, now a part of the nation of Oceana. There
are three major civilizations remaining on this planet, and
only three, despite the hundreds of nation-states of your
time. The strongest at this time is Oceana, comprised of
areas once known as Australia and New Zealand. Xhao-lin,
which you would have called northern China and Siberia is
almost as powerful, and prides itself on being the most
aggressive politically. Finally, Canalaska, made up from
Alaska and Inuit areas of Canada, is an up and coming
power, but began its redevelopment later than either
Oceana or Xhao-lin. Another developing area of
civilizations exists at the southern end of what you called
South America, but while it has a significant population, it
has no effective central government yet and no global
political power. The rest of the world was almost
completely destroyed, as well as virtually all civilization as it
was known in your time, in the year 2078 by McMurdoc's
Folly. How McMurdoc almost singlehandedly destroyed
the world is also a story for another time; suffice it to know
that 2078 was followed by 100 years of world-wide
barbarism, savagery, and intense suffering. That era was
followed by another roughly 100 years of regional isolation,
followed by 100 years of relearning what had previously
been known before the Folly, and then finally 50 years of
developing technology and global interactions, both old
and new, including the formation of the governments of
the three civilizations and interactions between the

governments".

"Because McMurdoc's Folly was caused by our own space-based nuclear weapons, the earth was discovered by alien sentient beings. These beings are composed entirely of energy; they travel the universe within energy fields they create and control, and are highly advanced compared to us on Earth. Indeed, without McMurdoc's Folly, they would never have found us for they would never have even looked at Earth".

"The energy beings exist at temperatures ranging up to, and exceeding, a billion degrees Celsius, as might be found in the center of stars. They isolate themselves in energy fields and travel through space at speeds faster than the speed of light by utilizing the contours of the time-space continuum to make folds that allow them cross light years almost instantaneously. They think and live at speeds that to us could be compared with the speed of light, only because we don't comprehend faster speeds". Rimu smiled a sly smile and continued, "So why didn't this advanced race of beings find us sooner and perhaps help us prevent McMurdoc's Folly?"

"Let me ask you, if you were going to look for other intelligent life, wouldn't you base your search for life on life as you know it, and set limits to your search if you reasonably could? Wouldn't you toss out the far extremes of whatever characteristics you might be searching? Let me use temperature as an example. We know the range of temperature we can measure goes into the billions of degrees Celsius at the top end. However, the bottom end, as far as we know, where all movement of atoms ceases, is at minus 273 degrees Celsius - the same as zero degrees on the Kelvin scale. The current temperature in this cave is just below 30 degrees Celsius or approximately 300 degrees above absolute zero - only 300 degrees from the absolute bottom of the temperature scale that goes up to billions of degrees. If one throws out the top 5% and the bottom 5% of the temperature scale, as we can measure it, to restrict our search for intelligent life, then we would have tossed out Earth as a possibility. In fact, we are such a frozen landscape that if you throw out only the bottom 1/1000th of one percent of the temperature range, Earth's temperature would still be far outside your search limits and would be excluded. The alien energy beings would not imagine anything living, much less sentient, on this frozen planet, where even our atmosphere would effectively be solid to them, and would not have considered even looking for life here. The activities of the energy beings are so rapid compared to us that they might live and die, with generations of their lives passing, before we could explain a simple math problem. They might grow old and die before we could even speak a poem. Why would anything, or anyone besides us, think that an environment so frozen, so solid, and at the extreme end of the spectrum of temperature could have sentient life?"

"But the detonation of more than 1000 nuclear weapons going off almost simultaneously on earth, coming from weapons that were launched not on the planet, but from near-space surrounding the planet, was sufficient to catch the attention of a traveling energy being." Rimu sighed heavily as if just speaking of this event was painful and tiring. Then he continued, "Clearly, something unusual was happening on this ice-like world. As the story was told to me", he said, remembering twenty years back, "the first attempt by the energy being to investigate Earth resulted in the incineration of everything the aliens tried to accumulate to study, since they lived at the high end of the temperature scale and we lived at the low end. So orbs were developed as an offshoot of the technology they use to enclose themselves when they travel through space and some were sent to monitor Earth. The orb is an energy field that surrounds and isolates whatever it contains. The field seemed to be what protects the energy beings as they travel through the cold of space, but orbs also contain and control energy equivalent to a small sun. Apparently, in the middle of a super nova or in the coldest, darkest corner of space, an orb would protect whatever it surrounded. So, for over 350 of our years, the alien energy beings have used orbs as a spy system to visit earth, to learn about us, and to report back to the energy aliens. However, we, as a world, knew nothing about the orbs or the aliens until just 25 years ago. You have held an orb, so you can understand why we might never have discovered something so small and transparent that was monitoring the earth. And perhaps we never would have known about the energy beings, if we had learned from our mistakes".

"As I told you, the world spent 350 years recovering from the nuclear holocaust of McMurdoc's Folly and only three civilizations have developed enough strength to sustain themselves. Only in the last 50 to 100 years were we able to return to the use of technology that is anything like existed before the Folly; but in some cases we have even moved ahead of technology that existed in McMurdoc's time, mostly because some old libraries and databases were re-discovered and much of the old knowledge had been preserved. But in our lack of wisdom, some of the newly developing political leaders determined that one of the first efforts to recreate the technology of the past would be to build a new nuclear weapon. The idea behind such a choice was that the first civilization to achieve this weapon could exert absolute power over others, since no other group could retaliate in kind. Twenty -five years ago, as the first new generation of nuclear weapon was being made ready to test, the alien beings intervened".

"On March 10<sup>th</sup>, twenty five years ago – now called Instruction Day, the leader of each of the three civilizations disappeared, each going missing simultaneously. Two were giving speeches before audiences when it happened and one was alone, but all three disappeared for most of one day. When they reappeared, they told of being in space, enclosed in an orb energy field, and of being studied and instructed by the energy beings – which were never seen. The orbs had monitored earth for 350 years, and even an exposure to an hour of our leader's time would be generations for the energy beings, so no one knows what they learned or inferred about us. However, the orbs provided communications in each of the leader's language and apparently each was told the same, or similar, things. First, the aliens said the inhabitants of Earth were, and continued to be, a war-like race and we would never again be allowed to possess nuclear weapons or even nuclear technology. Their orbs had scanned the earth to find sites of nuclear development and two days following the return of the leaders to earth, those sites would be removed. Each leader was instructed to evacuate people from all nuclear development sites within the two-day grace period. Second, the aliens would give each developing civilization an orb, which would provide sufficient energy that nuclear technology would never be needed on Earth. The orbs would be able to provide enormous assistance to the developing civilizations in other, not defined, areas, but would also continue to monitor the civilizations and inform the alien beings of the status of each civilization. The orbs could not be destroyed, or altered, despite how fragile they seem, and while they would respond to our requests, they were under the ultimate control of the energy beings. Third, the aliens would not interfere with Earth's development again as long as we did not attempt to export war off the planet. McMurdoc's Folly had been caused by the launch of over 1000 spaced-based nuclear weapons, and this seems to have been sufficient to be interpreted as moving war off the planet. And fourth, we would never be allowed to contact the energy beings; they would contact us if necessary, but we should assume that if the aliens felt that was necessary, that would not be good news for us. We were only a curiosity to the aliens; a new warring race, of low intelligence, in its infancy, to be allowed to destroy ourselves if we wished, but not allowed to export war beyond the planet. The glacial rate of our movements and development would never, throughout all of time, present any danger to the energy beings."

"The orbs also described to the three leaders a little about the alien beings. They are entirely energy, have no fixed shape, and control what we would translate as the dark energy of the universe – a force that makes up 70% of the universe and drives the expansion of the universe. The energy beings have a recorded history of over five billion years and throughout that time have had no interest in individual stars, much less planets, but see the purpose of their existence to guide the expansion and energy balance of the universe."

"Each civilization's leader was returned to exactly the same spot from which they disappeared. Each now possessed an orb they did not have when they went missing, or what you, Dr. Hart, call a sphere. A fourth orb was entrusted to the leader of Canalaska to be given to the leaders of the South American civilization seventy years hence. The leaders of Oceana and Canalaska both evacuated all nuclear development sites, but the leader of Xhao-lin did not. Military and site-workers were posted all over their nuclear facilities to protect them. Cameras recorded for history the events that followed two days after the leaders reappeared. A green line from the sky, originating from nothing that could be seen, swept over each nuclear site. The facilities simply ceased to exist as if they had been reduced to atoms. No humans were injured by the direct effect of the green line, but many were killed or badly hurt when they fell from where they had been standing on structures to the bare earth below, as the structures simply disappeared beneath their shoes."

"Since the removal of all nuclear development facilities, civilizations worldwide have taken as a fact that the alien instructions were real. It is universally accepted now that we have had contact with an alien intelligence, but we do not expect such contact to be repeated any time soon. It is accepted that the ramifications of exporting war beyond our planet would be disastrous. But the human race is a slow learner. Although we have now forsaken nuclear weapons and the race for space-based weapons, political leaders still crave greater power and so have now focused more strongly on control of all people on Earth, assuming that as long as nuclear weapons and space are not involved, any other atrocities will not invoke extraterrestrial intervention."

"At the time of the Instruction Day, the leader, or

Prime Minister, of Oceana was Rooka Tinboc, the father of our present day Prime Minister, Turook Tinboc. The names of the leaders of the other civilizations at that time are not important, since they would shortly be dead. Rooka Tinboc was a brilliant, but evil, man. For 10 days after the destruction of the nuclear facilities, he locked himself away with the orb he now possessed and experimented with it day and night. He learned he could order the orb to create the green line to scan and survey anywhere he wanted, and could cause the orb to deliberately destroy or obliterate materials, either killing or not affecting anything living. Later he would learn to kill with the orb, and to do it either directly or indirectly. He was able to draw power from the orb to make vast amounts of electricity. He could send the orb to other locations and call it back with just mental commands. And he found that his orb could scan the orbs possessed by the other leaders to learn for what purpose the other orbs were used. This last capability terrorized Rooka Tinboc, because he assumed that other leaders would soon learn that they could look through their orb at what Rooka was doing with his."

"And so the crafty old Tinboc organized the "World Unification Council" and invited each of the leaders of the existing civilizations to Oceana with the promise of demonstrating a method to use the powers of the four orbs to produce a world-wide system of clean and endless energy. He promised the other leaders would all share the credit for the greatest advance in peace and security since the beginning of time and that word-wide media coverage of such an advance would ensure each leader sufficient gratitude and respect from their people to keep them in power for a lifetime. At that time, the southern tip of what had been called South America was not a sufficiently organized civilization and the orb for that geo-political area had been entrusted to the leader of the Canalaska civilization until such time as a leader of the unified "'Southland" government had emerged. Tinboc requested that each civilization bring its orb (including the Southland orb) and he would illustrate the linkage of the four orbs for unlimited power. As you might expect by now, Tinboc was not well trusted, despite the promises he offered. Each leader came, but was escorted by guards and security unlike anything seen in hundreds of years. Independently, each of the civilizations even produced glass replicas of their orbs and only produced their actual functional orb when required for the power linkage. However, Tinboc put on a masterful event and, as promised, demonstrated the ability to link the orbs to create a worldwide power source. He was gracious and projected only the desire to see universal development and peace; and the event was reported the world over as the greatest progress of centuries. Remember, this was only 25 years ago, and the orbs are even now still new to us."

"However, Rooka Tinboc was not as magnanimous as he let on. Following a last press reception where the leaders made a point of showing the orbs being placed in the safekeeping of their respective security cases, in the care of each leader, Tinboc hosted a private meeting with only the two other civilization leaders, allowing only two trusted body guards each. Later, what the press, and thus the world, saw was that each leader, accompanied by two body guards, and Rooka Tinboc himself, boarded Tinboc's official government plane (Oceana One) for the flight back to Xhao-lin. Twenty-five years ago, only Oceana and Xhao-lin had reliable air transportation, so the arrangements were for Xhao-lin to bring the leaders and their parties to and from Xhao-lin, and for Oceana to provide transportation from Xhao-lin to Oceana. Four planes left that afternoon in a convoy. One plane carried the leaders and selected bodyguards, another plane was a fighter plane assigned to provide protection, and the remaining two were passenger planes containing the support groups accompanying the leaders – one plane dedicated to the press and security teams from Xhao-lin and the other plane with the folks from Canalaska. Three of the planes would land safely, but the plane carrying the leaders and their orbs would never be seen again. Sometime later, the government of Oceana would release a copy of a distress call from Oceana One; it was very short and beyond identifying the flight, offered only the word "Mayday", repeated twice, and a location fix. The three other planes had searched the area for wreckage until both dark and fuel requirements made continuing impossible. They found nothing and it was assumed the plane crashed in the ocean and all hands and 3 of the 4 orbs were lost, since Tinboc had left his orb under guard in Oceana."

"Ten years later", Rimu continued, "I would learn what really happened. The leaders of Xhao-lin, Canalaska, and Oceana had never boarded the plane. Rooka Tinboc had arranged body doubles for the leaders, including himself, and for the two security guards each leader brought to their last meeting. At that meeting he had each of the other leaders and their bodyguards killed and hidden. The look-alike leaders, and their security doubles boarded the plane, each group of three men from Canalaska and Xhao-lin carrying with them fake orbs. The press corps had been kept at a sufficient distance that no one ever suspected the men who boarded were not who they were thought to be.

It appears likely that the men who were on that plane were told to expect a different ending to the flight than actually occurred. Rooka Tinboc sacrificed the plane and all lives aboard when it was blown up over the ocean. The mayday message and location were both fake and the other three planes searched, of course, in the wrong place. But Tinboc was also now presumed to be dead. He needed to disappear, as did the three orbs that were supposedly lost at sea. And the dead bodies of the real leaders and bodyguards had to be more permanently hidden".

Rimu took a drink of water and settled more comfortably in his chair before the story began again. "Tinboc knew the success of the Unification Council meeting plus the sympathy of his supposed death would ensure the subsequent election his son, Turook, to lead Oceana. And that is exactly how events played out. Only now the two Tinbocs controlled all four orbs and Oceana was the undisputed world leader, being the only civilization with a remaining orb since the Rooka Tinboc imposter was known to not have taken Oceana's orb with him on the plane. Turook was now Prime Minister and Rooka, after cosmetic surgery, became an elusive advisor and the power "behind the throne", until he died of a heart attack about ten years later".

"You may wonder how I have learned these things. It turns out that the hiding place for bodies and other secrets would also become the location for the regime's political prison. One of my first discoveries when I initially arrived at Tenaru, was a cave containing a number of coffins. The bodies in those coffins supplied a missing portion of the story of which I only knew a tiny part. Other parts of that story I had learned earlier would result in my self-imposed exile to Tenaru. You should know that officially I am considered dead. Only those on this island know that I continue to draw breath, and you have seen the consequences of Thimlomarium, so I have little fear of being exposed".

"I, myself, benefited from the change of regime from Rooka to Turook, as I was advanced from a regional senator to Second Minister. For years I served as Turook's right hand man. My wife, also in politics, was far more insightful than I and recognized the moves initiated by the Tinbocs, moving us away from democracy and toward dictatorship, much earlier than I. But the seeds of doubt and awareness she planted in my mind grew over the years, and eventually Turook and I were getting pretty wary of, and concerned about, each other. The inevitable consequence of our mistrust took only twenty-four hours to come to fruition and change everything".

"Over the years as I worked with Turook, his office became the most secure area in Oceana. With the one exception of his advisor, no one entered Turook's office if Turook was not present. Keys to the office were limited and counted weekly, which was not difficult to do since there were only four. Turook, Rooka (the elusive advisor), a trusted cleaning person (who was my disabled cousin), and Turook's executive secretary (whom Turook required to log every entrance to the office) had the only access keys. I was never in that select group of key-holders. A secret electronic counter also logged the number of entrances to the office, and there would be hell to pay if the electronic and paper logs did not agree. While Turook traveled and managed the work of state, Rooka (in the guise of an advisor) would often enter the office to experiment with the orbs that were hidden there. So it happened one evening, while Turook and I were attending a press function, that in the middle of his speech Turook was alerted to some alarm from his office. Not wanting to create interest from the national press, he gave me his key and told me to check his office, leave it locked, and report back to him and return the key. I returned to the office immediately, wrote a short note for the secretary (who had gone home) giving the time I was entering the room, and let myself in. The shock I would get was not that a surprise was waiting, but the number of surprises in the room. First, I found a man dead on the floor and recognized him as Turook's advisor (Rooka). Second, he had the orb in his dead hand. I say THE orb because I believed there to be only one remaining orb. Third, a massive safe was open in the wall of the office and there was another orb or replica sitting in the vault. But the biggest surprise was that inside the open vault of the safe was another safe-within-a-safe that was also open. In the inner safe was a cradle clearly made to hold five orbs. The first spot was labeled MASTER and was empty. The second, third and fourth spots contained orbs and were labeled, respectively, XHAO-LIN, CANALASKA, and SOUTHLAND. The fifth spot in the cradle was labeled REPLICA and was empty. Apparently, Rooka had his massive heart attack just as he was taking out one of the orbs and had been unable to return it or close either safe door. The number of orbs was a dilemma for me until I realized that if these orbs were real, then they had not been lost at sea and so hypothetically Rooka had not been lost at sea either. It immediately made sense that Turook would not give one of his precious keys to anyone he did not trust completely, so the advisor was likely to be his father, Rooka Tinboc, and the dead man's build, although not his face, confirmed that as likely. It was unlikely that Rooka would experiment with a replica orb, so the one in his hand would most likely be the orb labeled as MASTER, and the orb so prominently placed in the outer safe would be the replica. Rooka and Turook were not stupid, but it seems they were rather unlucky on this day".

"Another thing that was quickly evident was that I was looking at information that had previously been shared by only two people on earth (one now dead), and as such, my life was going to be very much at risk if it became known how much I had guessed. In that moment, as a very real terror began to overtake me, I could initially see only two choices. I could return the orb Rooka had taken out and close both safes and pretend I had never seen inside either, or I could try to foil their plot and steal all the orbs. The latter plan would clearly point to me as the thief and the chances of me not being found out were small at best. But I was spared acting on one of those two ideas by the thought of a third option that might buy me more time. I took the orb from Rooka's hand and put it in my pocket. I then moved the orb from the outer safe (touching it only with my coat so as not to leave prints) and placed it in the cradle space marked SOUTHLAND. Each other orb was moved as well so that the Xhao-lin orb was in the spot marked MASTER, and so on leaving the REPLICA spot empty and with the real replica in the SOUTHLAND cradle space. That left the spot in the outer safe empty as well, but if the orbs in the MASTER, XHAO-LIN, or CANALASKA spots were checked, they would be real and powerful. Turook would not admit to anyone that he had all the orbs, and if he thought that the one missing was the replica from the outer safe, he might be slow or confused in his thinking since two people had been in the office that night and he could not ask Rooka what had happened. Once I had changed the orbs positions, I closed the inner safe and found it was carefully designed to be invisible, with no sign of any opening mechanism. I closed the outer safe door and moved the dead man that I now believed to be Rooka, closer to the desk. I locked the office door, and on my way back to report to Turook, I hid the Master orb I had taken in a janitor's closet in the basement of the building. I reported that the advisor had been found dead in his office, near to the desk, but that all seemed to be in order and I returned the key. Turook left the engagement immediately and returned to his office".

"The next morning a tired looking Turook announced he wanted to change the locks on his office. All four existing keys were readily accounted for, since Rooka had his on his person the night before. Then, unexpectedly, Turook sent his secretary home (I was later to learn that she never returned) and invited me into his office. I immediately noticed that the outer safe was open and an orb was prominent in the position I had left empty the previous night. He gave me some papers to review, sat me at his desk, and excused himself to run an errand and left the room. Since he had never left me alone in his office before, I was more than a little nervous, particularly since he had clearly left the safe open on purpose. But only a minute or so after Turook left the room, my cousin, the cleaner, happened by. Seeing the door open, and having just given up his key to the room, he stopped in to collect the trash. I stood to shake his hand, thinking how similar we looked this morning, even to the clothing we wore. Only our coats, his cap, and his limp distinguished us, but even so it was clear that we were family. However, in turning toward him I fumbled some papers and my pen onto the floor. We both bent to collect the papers and he reached for my pen. As he came to the level where I had been sitting, a silent blast of energy was emitted from the orb. The brightness and suddenness of the blast caused me to drop to the floor and peek around the desk to check on my cousin. At first he seemed fine, but then I realized that his head was missing. It had simply been atomized and cleanly removed from his body. The blast had been meant for me, and only luck had saved me. Turook had deliberately left the room, perhaps not being comfortable with his ability to control the blast from the orb, or wanting an alibi. I had been the target, but the blast had cost my cousin his life. As quickly as a man possessed, I switched coats, put on his cap (which had been in his hands), and gave the dead body all my personal effects, taking his. Without a word, I walked out limping, with my head down, although I saw no one, to the basement janitor's room. I hid in the basement all day and watched as they brought the body they thought to be me to the basement, and placed it in a flag-covered casket that was waiting. Turook and a man I did not know talked of sending the casket the next morning to Tenaru, 'with the others' were his exact words".

"The death of my cousin (thought to be me) had put the building on alert and, for me, getting out of the government building was now going to be difficult. To make a long story short, I spent the night modifying the coffin, with air holes under the flag cover, modifying latches I could open from inside, and cutting screws so, while they looked fully tightened, they were too short to fasten the lid. Then I recovered the hidden orb and climbed inside with the dead body and tightened the lid from inside. The wood was heavy and I am small; who would notice. I would be disappearing without a word to my wife or daughter, who would consider me dead. It was very painful, but I knew if I stayed I would in fact be quite dead soon enough. Apparently, I was transported, by an orb, to another part of this cave on Tenaru. When I emerged for the coffin, I found other coffins and the official state clothing and sashes of the "other dead" told me immediately who two of them were. It was not hard to fill in the blanks from there. More importantly, my luck continued to hold, not only was I officially dead, but Tenaru would become the political prison and among the first of the political prisoners would be my wife and daughter. After the shock of finding me alive, we had ten more years together before my wife died of the same symptoms that almost took Hanish. We spent those ten years watching after the folks sent here and studying the orb. Now I am teaching Hanish about the orb. But we will be able to do little against the regime until we can eliminate the Thimlomarium from our diet, so our first effort is to farm enough food, free of the chemical, that we do not have to eat what we are sent. The tenants of Tenaru are smart people, leaders before being sent here, but controlled by the Thimlomarium. And we must have them back to themselves before we will have sufficient wisdom and strength to move against the existing government".

"Still, we have an ace up our sleeve, as the gamblers say; we have the master orb. It is not known if Oceana was originally given the master orb, or if Rooka or Turook realized one was a master and took it as Oceana's. In any case, the master can influence the others, while the other orbs cannot influence the master in the same ways. It is my thought that the master gathers information from the others and reports to the energy beings, but who knows what is really true. Since it was marked "master" in Turook's safe, I immediately investigated and instructed the orb to influence the other orbs to allow the current Oceana orb to act as if it were a master orb, but to inform me of all "master" orders. I can then send back the information I want Turook to have. I still believe Turook does not know that the master orb is the one missing. In any case, I have been able to prevent the other orbs from finding this one. Each month I learn some new power of the orb and the difference between the master and the others. But I know Turook also studies these powers and he is ruthless and relentless; if he finds the location of this orb, there will be no living people remaining on this island".

"You should know that I was experimenting with the orb to see if it could go to a time before McMurdoc's Folly. I was hoping there was a way to change history and avoid the Folly, but I have only succeeded in making a mess of it, and involving you. I had not expected to find a person come back with the orb. Indeed, it was intended to go into what I thought was historically an unpopulated wilderness. You also need to know that I believe only if you are holding the orb, or touching someone holding the orb, will it transport you. But I am not sure of this since I have never transported people before. So you would need to carry your dog when we send you back or I cannot be comfortable that you will end up together – and again, I cannot be even sure of that".

Rimu continued a discussion of politics and the growth of Tenau as a prison. "But now I'm tired", Rimu said through a yawn. "Let's continue this conversation tomorrow evening. We will make the arrangements to send you back to your time and I will ask you to consider if you are willing to return here once the Thimlomarium is cleared from your system.  We would ask your help in freeing our people from Thimlomarium, but I cannot, and will not, force you."

# Chapter 5

## The Joys of Administration

Now I'm awake; I'm back in my nursing home room with my body still frozen in place. I woke when it was the middle of the night and I had to wait until morning to write down my thoughts. When morning came and I was moved to the computer, the calendar that the attendant here updates each day told me that weeks were missing from my memory. It is now late December and snow is deep outside my window. Not only can I not move, I'm forgetting weeks of time.

Once I am placed at the computer table, my machine turned on for me, and my hands placed on the keyboard, I am able to type and I am also able to read about Tenaru and the last several weeks that are missing from my memory. Initially, I believed none of it and wondered where the writing had come from. It doesn't cross my mind that this strange story has anything to do with me since I have no memory of anything I read about Tenaru and orbs.

I wish I knew how long I have been here; it doesn't seem very long to me, but the way folks work with (on) me, and ignore me, seems to suggest that they are very familiar with the routine. I overhear more talk of a stroke and a new doctor that will exam me. I'm not much help since I don't seem to be able to speak. But damn it, I've got a stake in what is happening to me and I'm still interested in what is going on. Since I can't ask, and precious little information is being given me, I've begun again to consider what I do remember and what might have happened to me that led to this situation. My thoughts keep coming back to my work at the University, the unreasonable administrative expectations, and how determined I was to make bad situations work, or at least try to turn them into something less bad.

It is funny, but I can't think of any single "worst" moment in my time at the University, it seems to be that the accumulation of events sum to a greater craziness than the individual parts. Could these events have led to such stress that I cracked up both mentally and physically? But even now my blood pressure is good, actually a little low. I hadn't, until I realized that I couldn't move, felt depressed. There were no warning signs that I can recognize even in hindsight.

As bad a shape as I am in, I must still have a sense of humor because I find myself laughing at the ludicrous events of some of the situations I experienced. Life is stranger than fiction sometimes, and, as they say, you couldn't make up stories this strange. I wonder if the craziness of my job, or perhaps a stroke, blew up my brain. My mind must be involved in my current problems, but I don't remember any singular event that would have put me here. I don't remember anything about an Orb, or Tenaru, or any of that, yet I remember my work. This is a story that came, unbidden, into my memory this morning.

As a dean, I was often invited (expected) to participate in fund raising events. This is even more the case when the purpose of the monies requested was in anyway for the benefit of a college or program that was overseen by any one of the deans. Our Dairy Science Department was lobbying hard for funds to build an organic dairy. Each year our College (Agriculture and Life Sciences) hosted a "controversial issues" symposium and brought in nationally known speakers to present opposing sides of a controversial issue. We had used one past symposium to consider the arguments around growing genetically modified organisms (GMOs) and the most recent symposium to consider organic versus traditionally grown foods. This had spurred the Dairy Science Department to want to construct an organic dairy. Since we already managed an existing traditional dairy, the thought was that an organic dairy would allow the Department to compare and contrast directly the benefits of each method for feed requirements (traditional confinement versus pastured, grass-fed), animal health (traditional vet practices versus no antibiotics and organic practices), and quality of milk (health benefits to people). At the time there was little real data or controlled research on these issues, as shown by the anecdotal quality of the presentations at our controversial issues symposium, and new significant research opportunities for the Dairy Science Department would be like a gift from heaven.

The down side was that we would need 2.5 million dollars to renovate an old farm the University owned, establish an organic herd, and hire staff to run it. The idea had received only lukewarm interest from the President and the Provost, until the University Advancement Foundation and a wealthy alumnus (owner of an international cheese plant) arranged for Utopia University to present its idea for the organic dairy (and solicit donations) at an international dairy foods conference. This conference had been organized, in part, by the wealthy alumnus to develop a twenty-year plan for the future of the cheese industry. All the big players in the industry were to be in California for this conference – Monsanto, Dean Foods, Aurora, Hood, CalAgra, and the list goes on. This once-in-a-lifetime opportunity to make a request for financial help for an organic dairy was too much even for our administration to overlook. I was selected to make the presentation and the President would go to "press the flesh" and show the level of commitment by Utopia University.

I used the time prior to flying down to California to pick the brains of our dairy faculty and prepare my talk. The day before we left, I presented the talk to the President's Executive Staff (where it was deemed acceptable with minor changes), picked up my suit from the dry cleaners, and packed my suitcase. As is my habit, I left the business suit in the plastic bag from the cleaners in case anything spilled or leaked in the suitcase. I thought I was ready.

The itinerary was for the President and me to fly to the LA airport, be picked up by our alumnus for a casual dinner, spend the night at his palatial home, and all attend the conference together in the early morning for my presentation. Utopia University was effectively an add-on to the conference and thus we were scheduled for 8:00am, prior the real business of the industry folks. The "casual" dinner turned out to be with two industry presidents, a government regulator, and the Governor's agricultural director, each with a spouse or partner. I was happy that I'd worn a sport coat on the plane and could, therefore, keep my suit unwrinkled for the conference presentation.

Following dinner, we returned to our host's house for a drink before bed. Last minute schedule changes (and the graciousness of our host) had over filled his bedrooms, leaving the host and his wife, two additional couples, and the Utopia president occupying the four upstairs bedrooms. I was relegated to a sleeper sofa in a sports bar/TV room at the bottom of the main stairs. After a pleasant evening, we all turned in, hopefully anticipating a productive next day. I was tired, and it felt good to get out of business clothes and into comfortable pajamas.

I'm a pretty light sleeper, so the first cry of "I'll get you, you devil!" brought me wide awake and onto my feet. The thundering of feet on the second floor caused me to run to the base of the stairs – just in time to see our president descending the stairs at a full speed – buck-naked and swinging a badminton racquet. Before I could say a word, he was past me, flailing the racquet and yelling, "Come back here you devil!".

Perhaps I should tell you a little about our president, to help you visualize the scene. This gentleman possesses a height of about 5 feet 8 inches and a weight of 240 lbs. As I was to learn that night, which was far too much information for me, he has bird legs and thin arms, poking out of a round body not unlike toothpicks in a marshmallow. On the stairs, his belly resembled the preverbal "bowl full of jelly", such that both big and little parts were bouncing around with no apparent control or coordination.

With a resounding, "God Damn you!" that I would learn later was not directed at me, the president was bounding back up the steps – Thump, thump, thump, crash! Then back down the steps came the bouncing belly and menacing racquet – thump, thump, thump, crash! This time I saw the dark shape of a bat and heard the wind from its wings as it flashed ahead of the racket with which our president was determined to "serve" it as a "birdie".

Another "I'll get you, you devil!" resounded off the walls. In the dark I could just follow the bat into my bar/bedroom and it disappeared behind a curtain. But my primary concern was for the expensive vases and lamps being fanned by the overactive badminton racquet. I was able to settle down the president, turn on a light, and see where the bat was clinging on the back of the curtain. I quickly gathered in folds of the curtain to trap the bat, took the rod off the wall and hurried the whole mass of material (and bat) toward the front door. On the way out of my bedroom, I noticed that there were towels at the foot of my bed (thoughtfully left by our host's wife) and I grabbed one for the President. Tossing it to him, I then carried the curtains and the bat outside to release the poor "devil". I returned inside to find three couples with mouths hanging open, at the bottom of the stairs looking at our president wrapped in a too, too little towel. If my thinking had been better, I might have ignored the towels, just to see where events might lead, but that would have been unkind. I still have nightmares about the president coming down the stairs full on, everything bouncing, with that racquet. It seemed at the time that nobody should have to witness that sort of spectacle.

Our host was truly horrified and apologetic over having a bat in the house and searched all the rooms to insure no others bats had taken refuge inside. Finding none, we all returned to bed, but sleep would not come, at least for me. What a day. We had put on quite a display and truly created quite an impression (read: story to be told over beers), but the main event was to be my presentation to the conference attendees and that was yet to come. Morning arrived and I remember thinking that at least this new day could not possibly be as embarrassing as the previous night. But once again I was wrong.

My presentation was to be the first event of the morning, but I only needed to shower and dress to be ready. My talk was on a "thumb drive" and I had been assured all the technology required to show my slides was in place. So I selected my best shirt, knotted my tie, and took my suit out of the plastic with which the cleaners had covered it. The creases were sharp and the coat looked new. I finished dressing and went to zip up the fly. I was still sleepy and hadn't had any coffee, but it slowly dawned that something was wrong. I couldn't find the fob that attaches to the zipper to let you pull it up. No, it wasn't that I just couldn't find it, there wasn't one. The problem wasn't just a missing fob, there was nothing to attach the fob to; half of the zipper was gone. One half of the interlocking mechanism that makes up the zipper was simply not there. There was nothing that could be zipped up. I had exactly ten minutes and we were leaving for the meeting. No coffee and no breakfast; Utopia University was providing breakfast for the attendees at the meeting (in appreciation of them coming to our event), so our plan was to get up, dress, and go. We would grab a bite at the venue. It was the "dress" part of that plan that was causing me problems. I quickly looked though the plastic bag the suit had been in for the missing part of my zipper (found nothing) and then the suitcase (found nothing). Then as panic set in, I looked for something to seal the gap. Every time I moved my pants opened to expose what my mind determined to be either the Grand Canyon or the Carlsbad Cavern. To make matter worse, I had on brand new white boxer shorts that showed though each gapping crevasse in my pants, like a flag of surrender on a battlefield of dark colored suit. I found a desk with a stapler and a single paperclip. It seemed that if I could just fix a "jury rig" until everyone got downstairs, someone would have some safety pins, so I stapled my fly closed and hooked the paperclip on the inside of the pants. But to my horror, it would turn out that not one safety pin existed in that enormous house. I resolved to forego coffee and not to urinate until the presentation was over, if necessary, so as not to disturb the fragile closure of my fly. I grabbed my notes and we were out the door headed to the car.

Just sitting down in the car pulled out the staples where the zipper was suppose to be and sent the paperclip shooting off inside my pants. The Grand Canyon had been re-discovered. Carlsbad Cavern plunged to new depths. The flag of surrender was visible for all to see. It didn't seem like there was any effective fix at hand, so I thought about asking the President to give the presentation for me. He had seen me give it once in practice. But it also occurred to me that since he had chased the bat while stark naked, he was unlikely to be very sympathetic just because I was having a "wardrobe malfunction".

My notes were in a Utopia University folder and I can say with certainty that I have never found a better use for one of those folders than I did that day. I sat with the folder in my lap; I walked with it in front of my crotch, I shook hands with my right hand and used my left to shield my fly with the folder. From my perspective, I was shamelessly flashing the world, but all others saw was a weirdo clutching a folder. It became my "canyon cover", my "cavern closure", and my "boner shield". When it came time for my presentation, I went through the words by rote, more interested in whether it looked like I was making love to the podium - I was standing so close. I never moved, I didn't fidget, and I will never "bad-mouth" the use of a laser pointer again.

At last it was over, and apparently the presentation was received very well. I was sitting under my strategically placed folder, thanking God that the presentation was finished, when I learned that at 3:00 pm that afternoon, I was to accept a gift from our host and that he would invite his colleagues to join him in supporting our organic dairy.

I just couldn't go through that again – making love to the podium and hoping that no one noticed. I sat unmoving until the lunch break and when the group went to eat lunch I made up a flimsy crisis I needed to deal with, excused myself and let myself out a side door. Using my smart phone, I searched Google for the location of a Chinese laundry. I caught a taxi, waiving my flag of surrender at the driver, and literally ran into the laundry with my ever-present folder. Having my pants washed would have been no problem, but I had to flash everyone in the store to make it clear that I needed a new zipper. Eventually they sat me in a chair behind a curtain that was not nearly long enough to hide my state of semi-dressed, and took my pants.

Over the course of the next hour I wondered if the proprietors understand what I had asked to have them do to my pants? It is not a comfortable position to be in a shirt and tie and coat, but no pants – even with a Utopia folder. I also wondered why it was that noon is the busiest time in a Chinese laundry. Maybe because everyone does errands at lunch, maybe it is a shift-change time, or maybe people just want to see someone without pants, but all sorts of folks burst behind my curtain, laughed and bowed, and backed out. Finally, the pants came back complete with a fully functional zipper.

I case you are interested, a rush job to get a new zipper on the pants you are actually wearing, under the conditions where you give them up to get them fixed and sit in a chair behind a curtain in a Chinese laundry, will run you about as much as five 25-pound bags of rice – a bargain at twice the price. I got back for the 3:00 appointment, accepted the first of several sizable donations that would eventually support our organic dairy, and worked the room with the freedom of a released prisoner until we left for home. I've often thought of framing that folder and putting it on my wall.

When I got home, my son asked how the meeting had gone. I told him, "Great, just another day in the office". But I have wondered, how does one protect against a situation like a missing zipper? I counted up the times that I had checked my clothes coming back from the cleaners to see if the zipper was missing. The number of times I had previously checked is none, zip, zero, nada, or didn't happen.

Our president never noticed my discomfort, or the problem with my pants, and I pretend to have never noticed that he was naked chasing a bat. So our working relationship didn't change at that point. Yep, it was just another day in the office.

## Chapter 6

## Rimu's Story: McMurdock's Folly

Sleep in our thatched hut at Tenaru came poorly, at least for me, as I tried to digest what Rimu had told me and thought about the new prospect of going home.  I got up in the night and wandered down to the river, with River, of course, following along.  The two of us sat on the edge of the dike we had helped to build and watched the stars.  I could feel the coolness of the night air, but a lot was beginning to make sense.  We were about to enter summer here, not winter as at home.  I knew the reason for the small rations of food, but knew nothing about the compound Thimlomarium.  I now understood that the sphere or orb had relocated us to another time and place, but I had no concept of what existed in the world beyond this island or the state of the rest of the world since the catastrophe that brought the earth to the attention of the energy beings.  I wondered what the energy beings wanted with information about earth, and why they had sent multiple spheres; that seemed rather unnecessary to me.  But it appeared the spheres could possibly send us (River and me) back.  And Rimu had promised to continue his story the next day (actually this evening since midnight had long past).  I gave up thinking and River and I returned to our hut, grateful for the sleep that finally came stealing over us.

That evening Hanish met us as she had promised and she and I and River returned to Rimu's home within the cave.  Again we ate before Rimu would continue his story, and again we had tiny servings of Thimlomarium-free food.

I suspected that due to the orb, as Rimu called it, much of current knowledge was far advanced beyond my experiences, but that following the horrific apocalypse Rimu had described, much of the sciences, in particular, might still be rather primitive in certain areas. I found myself wondering, as we ate, if Thimlomarium could be extracted from the food delivered to the island, since it had to be deliberately added at some point. I'd have to ask Rimu if the "spiked" food was grown with the compound or if it was added later.

Rimu took what was clearly his customary chair by the fire; Hanish put the green cloth over his lap and legs, and brought him a glass of water. He reminded me of myself preparing to give a lecture. His manner suggested that he was not expecting to be interrupted unless necessary for clarity or for him to impart a full understanding, and so questions should wait until the end. I'd assumed a similar position myself any number of times when I taught. But now I was the student with a hundred questions I wanted to know about, and I wanted the answers to what I thought was important to be answered first. I'd have to rethink if my old lecture style was the best way to teach or if I should open my lectures to questions from start to end. River didn't care one bit about Rimu's style since Hanish sat by him, giving the dog most of her attention.

The next part of the story poured forth from Rimu, with no interruptions for a substantial time. "It is important for you to understand a number of things about not only Tenaru," said Rimu, "but what happened to our world since your time over 350 years ago". "Since I intend to ask for your help, it is necessary for you to realize the situation we are in, why it has gotten as it is, and what options might exist to help the people of Tenaru. I shall start with the event we call McMurdoc's Folly and that will set the stage, as they say, for our future discussions. As you already know, in the year 2078, the earth was almost destroyed, resulting in a hundred years of the most difficult and barbaric existence for those still living, before any real recovery began. A bloody time that was, by Jove. Even now, whether you found yourself in Tenaru or elsewhere, you will find no domesticated, what do you call them, 'pets', I think. A few types of dog or cat-like animals may exist wild in some parts of the world, but for the most part they became extinct from over-hunting and being eaten. Hanish has never seen such an animal as your dog, and I have seen them only in historical videos. Very few wild animals exist now. We have a few wild deer on Tenaru, since we are effectively a wilderness, but most live beyond the Forbidden Pass. However, I digress, so back we must go to McMurdoc's Folly."

"Gregor McMurdoc was a brilliant young man in 2050. His principle skills were in computer programing and it was for those skills that the International Security Branch (ISB) of the United Nations hired him. He had trained in Scotland and Ireland and in the Silicon Valley of California, USA. He subsequently became a US Citizen and moved to the suburbs of New York to work for the United Nations. He was a diligent, tireless, and talented worker, showing no interest in political activism. His rise through the organization, from one position to the next of even greater importance, was meteoric."

"During the year 2059, following an exchange of nuclear missiles between Iran and Israel, alliances and treaties supporting each of the warring countries threatened to escalate the conflict into a world-wide nuclear conflagration with the potential to end all life on the planet. As retaliatory strikes were being planned around the world and, in the absence of any acceptable, face-saving plan for a resolution, it seemed almost universally accepted that the world was within perhaps only days of massive destruction. At this point, Gregor McMurdoc offered his suggestion. He proposed that the newly built, but not currently manned, International Space Station, be converted into a space-based weapons platform for deterring future aggression. According to his plan, each country could equip the platform with nuclear weapons (10 per country) to be aimed at designated targets. However, the launch of those weapons would be controlled by computers, programed and maintained by the International Security Branch of the United Nations. All land-based nuclear weapons were to be destroyed and in the event of any cheating or future nuclear weapons detonations, the perpetrator would automatically receive the space-based weapons targeted to it by the country attacked. No other country's weapons could or would be involved. Any attack with nuclear weapons would mean automatic retaliation in kind, such that any benefit from the attack would be rendered moot."

"So serious was the situation at that time that McMurdoc's proposal was accepted almost immediately by all nations, and overnight, the International Securities Branch of the United Nations became the most powerful organization on earth. The ISB was given access to the third generation of space shuttles, which allowed the ISB to quickly and efficiently convert the space station into a weapons platform and install over 1000 pre-targeted nuclear weapons. The United Nations oversaw the elimination of all land-based nuclear warheads, with universal political support. McMurdoc, who became head of the ISB, was considered a hero and often thought of as the most powerful and influential person on earth."

"But McMurdoc, himself, was quietly becoming more and more anti-war and began to fear the existence of over 1000 nuclear weapons, even under his control. And since many nations were at that time capable of near-space travel, he became fixated on security for the space station/weapons platform and arranged for international approval to arm the platform in order to protect it from any kind of attack imaginable. For over 15 years, peace was maintained on earth and prosperity was enjoyed widely; the world attributed this all to the presence of McMurdoc's space-based weapons and their anti-war deterrent."

"Time diminished none of McMurdoc's intellect or brilliance, but he became more introverted and paranoid. In 2075 he physically moved to the weapons platform in space and, along with only two personally selected colleagues, they ran the deterrent weapons operation with increasingly less international or United Nations input. Even the security features of the platform became increasingly secret, with weapon and security parts delivered on separate shuttle flights and assembled by McMurdoc and his two colleagues. It would happen, one year later, than an unsophisticated despot named Kim jun-ik, the leader of North Korea, financed an attack on the weapons platform with the intent to blackmail the rest of the world and increase his importance. A specially trained commando unit hijacked a scheduled supply shuttle, but when they reached the vicinity of the weapons platform and could not complete the security procedures, they were told to "stand off". The hijacked shuttle had rigged and was able to fire a powerful laser weapon at McMurdoc's station and began an approach to board the platform. That shuttle was annihilated by the weapons platform's defenses. As news of this attempted attack spread around the world and the population of North Korea rose up against the tyrant and killed him; nations praised McMurdoc's preparations, and the budget for the weapons platform was massively increased. While the weapons installation was not damaged in the slightest, McMurdoc now felt that his concern over the presence of such a huge stockpile of weapons had been confirmed. And that set in motion the events leading to 'The Folly'."

"The next two years leading into 2078 saw frantic activity and intensified secrecy aboard the weapons platform. Then on December 10th of 2078, McMurdoc sent his two colleagues back to earth on an autonomous supply shuttle for a three-week holiday vacation, choosing to remain aboard the platform alone. There was nothing unusual in this; the surprise would come five days latter on Dec 15. After securing the weapons platform and activating all the defense mechanisms on board, McMurdoc made coffee and took his seat in the main control room chair. He then broadcast, on all media (and military) frequencies, his demands. Nearly the whole world watched in real time as McMurdoc expressed his fears of having exactly 1230 nuclear weapons, even under his watchful eye in a presently secure location. Time would certainly change nation's capabilities and aspirations. The presence of such a nuclear force as the weapons platform would be too great a temptation at some point for some to resist and he, McMurdoc, could not protect it forever. The better solution would be to destroy the stockpile of nuclear weapons and allow the International Security Bureau to devise a new non-nuclear deterrent. He would insist, since he could not change the targeting of individual missiles, that each county with weapons on the platform alter the targeting of each missile to the center of the sun by Christmas day. He would then launch all of the weapons into the sun, ensuring their destruction without harm to anyone. He knew, of course, that not all countries wished to give up their nuclear armaments, but to make their decision easier, McMurdoc promised that if all weapons were not re-targeted by noon on Dec 25th, he would launch all 1230 weapons at their current targets – an action that, in his opinion, would only speed up an inevitable consequence. McMurdoc explained that indeed he could launch all the missiles, since he had built a "backdoor" into the weapons platform computer programing that gave him such ability. He was, within 24 hours, going to initiate a program to command the launch of all the missiles at their existing targets and that only he could countermand the programing order. He would block any attempt to have anyone board or threaten the weapons platform, and the world, therefore, had no choice but to retarget the missiles or die because of them. He ended by saying how much he looked forward to launching all the missiles into the sun on Christmas day and to the start of an era without nuclear threats."

"Now, the world leaders, as is often their style, would not condone blackmail. They ordered a fleet of non-nuclear missiles to be directed against the weapons platform, but the defenses of the platform were easily up to the task of destroying the entire group. McMurdoc responded by initiating the launch sequence and displaying to the world a countdown clock showing the remaining time until all 1230 missiles would be launched at their earthly targets. The seven most advanced nations then each, simultaneously, sent a modified space shuttle to destroy the entire weapons platform. At one command, five of the shuttles fired laser weapons at the platform and two launched nuclear-tipped missiles (which all nations swore they did not have). In response, seven simultaneous laser beams erupted from the platform, neutralizing, and then pushing the weaker laser beams emanating from the shuttles back into those ships, while the missiles were detonated within 100 yards of the ships that launched them. The result was complete destruction of the shuttle fleet by a totally automatic platform defense system. One clever nation notified McMurdoc that it had retargeted the first 5 of its missiles to the sun and would like for McMurdoc to launch them early to show that some nations were willing to destroy the weapons. However, when McMurdoc checked the trajectory given these missiles, he found that they headed initially toward the sun but were programed to return to the coordinates of the weapons platform where they were to detonate. McMurdoc gave credit for a good try, but promised if the retargeting was not done properly to go to the sun for detonation, then the first weapons to hit the earth would land in that clever nation."

"By this time it was Dec 22. Three days remained before McMurdoc's deadline. As usual with politicians, the negotiation would go on to the last minutes, even if there were nothing to negotiate. McMurdoc pleaded for swift action, that the good of the whole must be considered above all else, and preached the benefits of a world free of nuclear weapons. He also assured everyone that there were only two options: nukes to the sun, or nukes to the earth.

He had the cancel order for the launch programed in and only needed to activate it once he was assured that the missiles were aimed at the sun. But time was getting short and the stakes could not be higher."

"On Christmas eve and Christmas morning he called on the people of the earth to contact their leaders and demand they comply. He said he had thought this through carefully, found no other way to peace, and had overlooked nothing. If the people would help him with his goal and pressure their leaders, he would come back to earth and face trial anywhere; but only once the missiles had been sent to the sun. This was to be his last message to the people of earth, he would now wait for word from world leaders that his demands were met."

"At 10:40am on Dec 25, 2078, the leaders of the world agreed to meet McMurdoc's demands. Word was sent to McMurdoc that he had won, the nations had all agreed to meet his demands, and retargeting would be completed within the hour, all prior to the noon deadline. His had been a brilliant strategy and he should now savor his success. But McMurdoc returned no reply. One moment McMurdoc was sitting in his control chair ready to active the cancel command, and the next moment he was dead. He had overlooked nothing, except his mortality. We are now quite certain that McMurdoc died of a massive cerebral hemorrhage due to an aneurism that burst. Alive one minute, dead the next. But the world didn't know this and for an hour and twenty minutes, the world waited as the automatic events on the weapons platform continued as programed. Concern grew as no response came from the platform, but nothing could be done in the time remaining. At exactly noon, 1230 nuclear missiles were launched toward the earth and the resulting explosions caught the attention of a traveling energy being."

"McMurdoc's Folly is ironic on so many levels. It didn't need to happen; it should not have happened; it was suppose to bring peace. I will not expound upon the suffering that resulted, but say only that new generations, at least every other generation, seem to need to revisit the sins of their fathers and relearn the hard lessons. The Tinboc regime is taking this world in a dangerous direction once again. The people on this island are the ones who would have opposed this danger, but now are made impotent by Thimlomarium, and our time is running out. I have the Master Orb, and I am being driven, like McMurdoc, to take the most dangerous steps to save us all. I have only Hanish to talk with about these things and she has only the experience of her life on this island (since she was fifteen years old) to draw on, although her common sense is excellent. I need you, Dr. Hart, regardless that your presence here is accidental, to understand our situation so I can test my theories by running them through your council, before I inadvertently create another McMurdoc's Folly."

At this point, I interrupted Rimu's story. "Rimu", I said slowly, "have you ever traveled through time?" His answer indicated that he had not. "Well, I never had either until I was brought here. Your story is amazing, overwhelming, and terrifying all at the same time. Of course I will try to help in anyway I can, but I wonder if my thinking is very clear; I seem to be still in a state of shock and the only thing I know is that I don't know very much about what is going on here or anywhere else, it would seem. First, Tinboc must know that one of the orbs is missing by now. Do you know if he is searching for it?

Second, why don't you just use your orb to travel back in time and kill McMurdoc before the Folly. And third, you can't do anything about Tinboc alone, so you need a way to get your people on Tenaru back to fully functional, and that means getting rid of the Thimolmarium. What do you know about the compound? Is it added, or are the crops grown in soil laced with the compound? Lastly, perhaps you could let me know what you can and cannot do with the orb, so I know what sort of dangerous things you are thinking about." I paused for a breath and because Rimu looked as if he wanted to say something. But the quiet extended for some time as Rimu considered, in silence, the questions I had presented.

Finally Rimu spoke, "Quite reasonable questions, it seems to me, and as good a place to start as any other. However, while I will tell you what I know, I am sure of very little and much of what I can tell you will be conjecture and educated guesses. But let us begin with Tinboc and the remaining orbs. Yes, by now he must be certain that one orb is missing, though I doubt he has much of a clue where it is. The Master orb can "record" commands to the other orbs and replay the actions taken. I have seen that Tinboc has used each of the remaining orbs and it seems certain that he is aware that only three of his four orbs are functional, and that one is a fake. Of course, he cannot admit that he knows this since he perpetuates the fallacy that three orbs were lost in the plane crash that supposedly killed his father. But he has instructed his orbs to watch for the tell-tail evidence of any other orb being used. I have been able to modify his command, using the Master orb, so that his orbs ignore actions of the Master, but faithfully report any use of his three orbs. For fifteen years this has been a successful ploy, but recently he has changed his commands to be more specific about what the other orbs should look for as they search for the missing orb. I have told you earlier that I think he still believes that he holds the Master orb. I have worked diligently to allow one of his orbs to act, through events and actions, in support of this delusion. Yet recently I have become concerned that he suspects some trickery. His is constantly changing search parameters, a new occurrence that suggests a change in his thinking, and this has me worried. I have made it a point to use the Master orb only deep within this cave, which I know to be safe from the probing of the green line, or, as was the case when the orb was returned from the past (your time), a full days walk away from this location. One of my men was sent to watch for its return, but he first went to the wrong location then a day later to the correct site. The day after you arrived on Tenaru, the green line appeared. A "green line" count had just been conducted the week earlier, and so no one was expecting it to return for another three weeks. It would seem that the green line was searching for something that correlated with the return of the orb. That, itself, is a major worry and I can only conclude it is an indication that the clever Tinboc is refining his game as he searches for the missing orb."

"The question of using time travel to go back to deal with McMurdoc, or for any other purpose, is easier for me to answer. But again, I have no direct evidence that what I will tell you is correct. However, there is a story from what we now call "Instruction Day" that the alien energy beings are reported to have told the three leaders that they abducted. To make a long story short, the reason that the aliens did not go back in time to prevent the development of new nuclear weapons capabilities on earth, rather than destroy what had been newly created, was that when one travels back in time, brain patterns (or whatever memory mechanisms are used) are lost, since those memory mechanisms had never been formed in the past. That is to say that one traveling back in time can remember nothing about the future they were part of. One would not know why they had gone to the past, moreover, they would not remember anything about the future. Anyone from a future further ahead than a lifetime would be as mindless as a baby and have to relearn everything. It was assumed that anyone returning to the past, from an old age in his life, to say, the middle age in his life, would retain knowledge up to that actual date in the middle of his life, but would know nothing of his old age. As far as I understand, these assumptions have not been tested since we have had the orbs; but there is great faith in what was learned on "Instruction Day" and these stories are believed without question. "

Rimu's seriousness, as he spoke, convinced me that he absolutely believed what he was telling me. But there was an implication to his story that I needed to clarify. "You're saying", I interrupted again, "that you can send me back to my time, but that I will not have any memory of being here, at all. Is that right?"

"Yes, that is my belief", said Rimu. "But that need not be too great a worry for you; we'll be able to carry on quite well enough. If you return to your time and then come back to our time, you should have all your memories of your time when you are there, and all the memories of our time when you are here. It is only in your time that you will not remember our time, nor will you remember the transition periods. But, you need only to be gone from here for twenty-four to thirty-six hours at a time, every few weeks, to clear any residual Thimlomarium."

"The Thimlomarium in our food here on Tenaru", Rimu continued, "is added prior to being delivered. We know what food it is added to by a slight green color left on the food, somewhat the color of dried peas. Cooking in water does not remove it. But until we can grow enough of our own "clean" food, we must feed the people here with what we are given. Toward that end, we have asked you to help with the construction of the new dike to prevent flooding. I intend that we will save as much of what we can grow this summer in the depth of this cave where it is cool, to allow us usable food in the winter. But I doubt there will be enough to free all of us from this diabolical chemical. This is particularly so since we receive, on average, two new political prisoners sent to Tenaru each month."

"Unfortunately, now is not the time to talk about the orb and its powers. To understand the orb, it is best to use it. But, as we have been discussing, Tinboc seems to be searching again for the orb, and I cannot chance that he discovers where it is – or that I am still alive. Hanish has been learning the working of the orb in case anything happens to me, and if you chose to help us and return to our time once the Thimlomarium is purged from your system, I will include you in the lessons of what I know about the orb."

We continued to talk well into the night about the political structure of Oceana, the island of Tenaru, the size and history of the prisoner colony, and the plan to send me back to my time to clear the Thimlomarium. We agreed to have Rimu return me to as close as possible to the truck, and I would return back to Tenaru after 24 hours. As time came to leave the cave, I asked for a sample of food that was spiked with Thimlomarium and was given a small sample by Hanish, with a stern warning not to eat any of it. Hanish offered to see us back to our hut, and as much as I would enjoy her company, I wanted to review what we had learned and think about the return to my time, and so River and I made our own way back to the village.

## Chapter 7

## Back at the Geezer Garage

I woke up in the middle of the night feeling very anxious, but can't figure out why I'm feeling anxious. It is clear that I'm still in the Geezer Garage (what I have taken to calling my uncomfortable room in this old folks home or nursing home) but there is nothing that I can think of that has been going on here that would cause me to feel this way. It has apparently been quite a few months, or longer, that I have been here, but my memory, which had always been pretty good, now seems to be going to hell in a hand basket. Most of the time that I have spent in the Geezer Garage (from the time I was admitted until now) I can't remember at all; sometimes weeks at a time are gone from my mind as if I slept through the time without even a dream.

I tried to remember what has been going on about me recently, but since the camping trip, the only time I can remember being anxious is when I'm unable to communicate with anyone, and at night there is no one to communicate with anyway. If only I could speak, I could probably get through this imprisonment in the Geezer Garage, since I could contribute my thoughts. And yet the irony is killing me, I can't tell you how many times I have said to myself that if only I could have kept my mouth shut, my life would have been so much easier. But that had never been my style – until now.

So why do I feel so anxious? It is not a feeling of dread, and there doesn't seem to be anything unusual here (that would be wishful thinking), but I know the feeling I have – something is going on, even though I don't know what it is. It is the feeling I get when something important is pending and I am not yet ready for it. It happens to me regularly when I have a presentation I need to give, or a particularly transitional lecture full of information important to understanding the concepts that are to follow, or anytime I have just one chance to get it right.

I also have a feeling in the pit of my stomach that when I get set up at the computer in the morning that there will be another chapter of the saga I am reading on it about my "adventures", of which I know absolutely nothing. Still, that is entertainment for me, the only new communication I get. So while part of me really struggles to make some sort of sense out of what I find written, another part of me looks forward to finding a new installment.

So what is ahead of me that makes me feel so anxious? God knows that I am no stranger to anxiety; but it has never before left me waking up in the night and staying with me so intently for no known reason.

Could anxiety be the cause of my paralysis? If so, it seems my problems should have started years ago. I can't help but remember the trip I made with the newly hired dean (coming to Utopia University from another college), up into the North Cascades, and our encounter with the bears. Now I've run into bears any number of times, and I have great respect for these powerful animals, but they have always gone their way and I have gone mine. Live and let live seems a good philosophy to me. One never knows when one might run across a bear in the mountains (their home), but the trip I'll describe had more bears per square mile than any trip I'd made before or after. And caused me more anxiety than any other trip.

Utopia University had hired a new Dean of the College of Liberal Arts. I had personally thought we should have hired the woman candidate, however that was not the search committee's choice, but I was happy to do what I could to welcome the newly arrived administrator. This gentleman had been deemed to be a good "fit" for our university, all things considered, and his support had been enhanced by his often-expressed love for backpacking and the northwest mountains. He was moving from a university in the south and our President and Provost wanted to be sure he would be made welcome. Thus it was that I was asked to take the new dean backpacking during some dead time in his moving schedule. Given that a bad day backpacking is usually better than a good day at work, I readily agreed. Since he was new to the area, I was left to choose the route. There would be plenty of opportunity later to travel the close-by areas, so I chose a three-day hike in the North Cascades, starting at the Thunder Creek trailhead. We would take my pickup truck with the camper and stay the first night at the trailhead. The night after leaving the truck we would need to pitch a tent, the second night we would stay in a three-sided forest service shelter (I assumed it would still be there after the ten years since I had last hiked that trail), and the third walking day we would complete the loop and hike out to the camper. That didn't seem too hard for this guy's first trip in the northwest mountains, if he was at all experienced.

As we prepared to leave from the university, I was a little suspicious of the amount of brand new "stuff" the new dean had. The brand new, never used hiking boots, however, should have been a dead giveaway. But off we went. The first night was uneventful, I enjoyed his company and some academic conversation, and the next morning we put on our backpacks and started off up the trail. He carried my 3-person tent with his pack and I carried all the cooking equipment, the food, and the tent poles. I knew I'd have more weight than normal for this trip, but I wanted Bob's (the new dean) trip to be enjoyable. That we were in for an eventful trip was obvious by three hours into our walk; we'd stopped at least four times "to catch our (Bob's) breath" and Bob had developed significant blisters on his heals. I doctored his feet with "moleskin" and loaned him a pair of thin liner socks and a pair of smart wool socks. About an hour later we saw our first bear, a Momma Black bear with cubs. She was well off the trail, but we gave her plenty of room and quietly walked by. I reminded Bob never to get between a momma bear and her cubs, or "spook" a bear unnecessarily, since it was then that they were most dangerous. Bob was pretty done in when we got to our first campsite so I set up the tent and set about cooking to give him a chance to rest. After a short walk for him to heed the call of nature, he told me that he had seen some animal at the edge of a meadow near us, and thought it might have been a bear or a deer. I wasn't comforted by his inability to know one from the other, but I assured him it wouldn't be a problem, we would just make sure to hang our food high in a tree, far away from the tent, that night. As an after-thought, I asked him to check that no food would be left in his pack or in the tent. He slyly produced two chocolate bars and a bag of trail mix from the tent, which I hung with the rest of the food.

We turned in early, after dinner, and both fell rapidly asleep. It was pitch dark when I was awaked by the sound of running feet outside the tent. I quietly listened as the steps ran off into the woods, and was just dozing back off, when they returned – running right up to our tent. By now, Bob and I were both awake, and I grabbed my flashlight from its customary place in the tent gear pocket, and unzipped the tent to look out. Directiong the light out the tent door, I found myself looking into the face of a black bear, about 10 feet away. I turned off the light and zipped the door closed. After explaining to Bob that it was a bear outside, I whispered that we should just be quiet and the bear would go away of its own accord. I don't know how but, even though it was pitch dark in the tent and the flashlight was off, I knew Bob was as white as a ghost. The bear decided to sniff its way around our tent, grunting and emitting a distinctly unpleasant bear smell. The next ten minutes were an eternity. But soon there was no further noise, so I looked outside again. Nothing there, the bear was gone.

We must have pitched our tent right on his path to the stream, I thought. No problem, the bear was gone and bears usually didn't want to be around people, any more than we wanted to be around them, so it was time to finally get some sleep. I suppose I slept an hour or two before the footsteps returned. This time, the running came again right up to the tent and the growling and sniffing started once more. As the bear sniffed its way around the tent in the dark, he became tangled in the lines holding the tent up and as he jerked away, the tent shook and danced like it was going to fall down. There was a low groan from Bob, so I told him to relax and just be quiet, the bear would check us out and then leave. But I didn't believe what I had just said; there was something wrong with this bear. They don't charge up to tents over and over; they shouldn't be too comfortable around people. Great, just my luck, we'd encountered a rogue bear. Another interminable time passed and then we heard the bear charge off a short distance and then there was silence. We listened, but all remained quiet. Bob wanted to leave camp immediately, right then in the middle of the night. I talked him out of that idea, suggesting that it was more difficult to hike with just headlamps for light and that if we ran across the bear (or any bear), we would be so close before we saw it that it could be dangerous. It was harder to talk him out of building a big fire and setting part of the forest on fire to chase off the bear. Apparently it didn't occur to Bob that the resulting forest fire that the bear would have to be worried about, would be something that we should also be worried about. I remembered at that point that I would have to be working with this dean for the foreseeable future, and it was not a comforting thought. I didn't sleep much after that (partly to be sure that Bob didn't decide to unilaterally start his fire after all), and I am sure Bob didn't sleep at all. We counted minutes to the dawn, but there were no more visitations that night.

The next morning we were out of the tent early, had coffee and instant oatmeal for breakfast, and were on our way up the trail by 7:00am. There was very little talk of the previous night until after about two hours of walking, we ran into a ranger doing trail maintenance. We told him our bear visitation story (leaving out the part about burning down the forest), and I mentioned the unusual actions of this bear, knowing the ranger would understand I was telling him there was a rogue bear, and that probably Bob would not. The ranger calmly told us that two days before, a nuisance bear had been trapped for causing trouble at the dumpsters in a car camping ground on the west side of the mountains, and had been flown over to this area (where there were few people, since the only way to get here was to hike in) so the bear could learn to be a wild bear again. Unfortunately, the bear, in my opinion, was a slow learner and actively hanging on to his old ways of expecting people to provide him food. Probably to make us feel better, the ranger said, "Well, it was a good thing you didn't have any goodies in your tent, cause he (the bear) would have come right in, and then you would have probably pissed him off".

Fortunately, we had "bearly" dodged that bullet.

No more excitement that day, just lots of rest stops, until we arrived at the three-sided shelter where we would spend the night before heading back to the truck. The shelter was three-quarters of an hour walk below the highest point of our last pass, so from here on out we would only have downhill to travel. The shelter was indeed still here and in remarkably good shape. It was dry and almost clean, but I swept out some little feces pellets with pine branches anyway. We hung a piece of plastic ground cloth over the open side of the shelter to keep out the wind and to try to retain our warmth since it got much cooler at this altitude after the sun went down. We had a leisurely dinner, swapped stories about our previous lives before coming to Utopia University, and watched deer grazing less than a hundred yards from our camp, before turning into bed right at sunset. Since neither of us had a very restful night the previous evening, we both felt we could use a good nights sleep. The last thing I did before getting in my sleeping bag was to re-stretch the plastic ground cloth tight across the opening of the shelter, and place a flashlight and cooking pot (in case I needed a noise maker) close at hand.

I think we were both asleep before our heads hit where a pillow should have been. But I have always been a light sleeper, and may have still been on edge from the night before, so when I heard the plastic sheet rustling, I came wide-awake and slowly grabbed the flashlight. Once it was switched on, the intruder was obvious; a large deer had poked its head into the shelter. As soon as the light was on, the deer turned and ran like the wind. Only the fact that she (the deer) had no antlers kept the ground cloth from being shredded. I was thankful for that small favor (since I wouldn't have to get out of my sleeping bag), as well as the fact that I didn't think Bob had even woken. I was back asleep in minuets.

Some time later, the plastic rustled again. Waking more slowly this time, I was sure the deer had returned so I haphazardly grabbed the flashlight and turned it on. This time there was a bear entering the shelter on my side where the plastic met the wall. In my surprise, I yelled "Hey!" The bear, acting as if it did not appreciate either me, or my flashlight, slowly pulled back out of the shelter and ambled off as if disappointed by a "no vacancy" sign. This time, my own doing had awakened Bob in time for him to see the bear.

Terrified would be a kind way to describe Bob at that moment. A little later, when I had 1) calmed him down some, 2) checked outside the shelter with the flashlight to ensure that no monsters lay in wait, and 3) re-strung the plastic cover, he asked what to do if the bear came back. I told him that I doubted that would happen again, but if a bear came in the shelter, he should just play dead. In truth, I really didn't know what to do, but to tell him something, and maybe to give him some false confidence, I told him that he should go so limp he would make a wet dishcloth look rigid by comparison. I'm still a little ashamed now that that was the best advice I could give him.

Needless to say, sleep did not come quickly to either of us. Some substantial time later I heard Bob's steady breathing, and relieved, eventually I fell back asleep. As you might have guessed, the plastic was rustled yet again. This time, there was a loud thump with the rustling, a short pause and then another rustling. I woke and thought, "Damn! What the hell is it this time". I slowly reached for the flashlight, but before my fingers found it, the bear's paw landed squarely upon my chest. Even through the sleeping bag, I could feel the claws working in and out slowly. I froze. All I could think of was "go limp, make a dish cloth look rigid", my own crappy advice to Bob. It crossed my mind to call out to Bob for help, but I didn't really think I could count on a whole lot of help and I didn't want to startle the bear. The claws just kept working in and out, like a cat does, but many pounds heavier. So I continued my dishrag imitation. I didn't know if Bob was awake and didn't much care; it was pitch dark, I was half asleep and I was certainly thinking slowly. I decided to wait it out; any attempt to escape seemed like it would have an excellent probability of getting me hurt or killed, maybe also endangering Bob. As I waited long minutes, it was my turn to be terrified. The only thing in my mind was the weight of the paw and the feel of the claws. More minutes passed, and neither of us moved. It was a like a game of chicken; who would be the first to break? I became more and more sure it was not going to be the bear that broke. I was decidedly afraid and losing my control. I wasn't going to last much longer. Finally, I decided I would get away or die trying. That decision helped, because suddenly I could make plans. I remembered the cooking pot and knew my right hand was already near the flashlight, but I could also still feel the claws and the slight movement of the paw on my chest. How fast could the bear claw me open if I tried to move? Would banging the cooking pot scare it off, or piss it off? Why had the ranger told me that if the bear came in our tent, then we would probably piss it off? It seemed obvious that a pissed off bear was not something you wanted close to you. Would it bite me, claw me, or both?

In desperation, I forced my hand to slowly find the flashlight. I had decided that at the same time I switched on the flashlight, I would grab the cooking pot and smash it against the bear or the wall and scream to scare the bear off. I was probably going to die.

It all happened in a heartbeat. The light came on, the cooking pot hit the wall and I screamed! Then Bob screamed! The claws worked deeper into my chest. The light filled the small space and illuminated, still on my chest, an extremely large, terrified Jack Rabbit, shaking and still working its claws in and out. It was as scarred as was I. As Bob's scream died out, the monstrous rabbit bound off me and was gone, leaving me trying to catch my breath. Once again, neither Bob nor I slept the rest of the night.

Things always seem less scary in the daylight. We laughed about the rabbit and the preponderance of bears on the trip, but both of us were faking it to some extent. After breakfast, Bob, despite having not slept much for two nights, put on his pack and did not stop once until we were back at the truck. We've become good friends since then, but he has never backpacked with me again.

I tell this tail because I wondered if anxiety could have put me in this old folks home. But I was as anxious on that trip as I have ever been, or want to be, when I had that "bear paw/rabbit" on me, and even that wasn't enough to drive to me to the Geezer Garage.

# CHAPTER 8

## Orb wars and the Forbidden Pass

When I opened my eyes, all I could see was Rimu and the forest. Rimu looked more worried than I had seen him since Hanish was so sick. I started to speak, but he interrupted, addressing me. "Are you hurt? Can you walk?" I had no idea where I was, but I cleared my mind and checked myself out. I seemed okay, so I got up on my feet and asked what was going on. Rimu quickly explained that I had just returned from a trip to let me clear the Thimlomarium from my system, but there had been a problem.

A problem? It seems so simple when you say it like that. What kind of a problem? What kind of trip and where had I been? Where was I now? Why didn't I know what was happening? But all those questions would have to wait; right now, my dog River was in my face licking me like I'd been gone for a week. I took him in my arms and rubbed his head. As soon as he calmed down, Rimu was encouraging me to get moving. He said that we had lots to talk about on the way back to the village. It turns out that was a whopper of an understatement.

We walked and ran, in turns, for almost five hours to get back to the village. The walking part of the trip back was only for my benefit and so we could actually talk. The rush back to the village was apparently due to a prediction by Rimu that a previously unexpected scan by the green line would occur shortly, within hours. In case we were caught by the scan, Hanish and a villager were hiding in a deep part of the cave, so that they would not be counted. This would mean that if Rimu and I were scanned, the number of inhabitants on the island would be consistent with other "counts". But Rimu did not know what information about individuals was collected by the scan - or if just numbers were collected. Rimu had never been scanned since coming to Tinaru, always hiding in his cave when villagers alerted him of a green line approaching. Likewise, I had never been scanned (having been protected by my boat), and Rimu wanted to keep it that way for both of us. As it turned out, we made it to the village an hour ahead of the green line scan, and when it came by, Rimu and I were safely in the cave, with Hanish and the villager back in the village. I found it interesting that Hanish always made an effort to be included in the scan, since she had been sent here as a child and was known to be one of the political prisoners. While we waited in the cave, expecting the scan, I learned that I had been sent back to my own time to clear the Thimlomarium from my system; in fact, I had been sent back to my own truck at the campground site on Marble Creek. I had told Rimu about the truck and camping trip as we discussed how I had arrived in Tenaru and when we spoke of sending me back he had apparently remembered and decided that the truck was an excellent hiding place for me, both remote in location and comfortable enough since it had a bed.

I hadn't seen the sphere since Rimu had magically made it move from my hand to his when we had first met, but all the way back to the village and even in the cave, he carried it prominently in his right hand and constantly seemed to be expecting something from it. I had learned on the way back to the village, that Rimu was in some sort of a contest or war with his rival Turook Tinboc. Turook apparently still thought Rimu to be dead, but a war of some sort was being played out through the spheres - even though Turook did not know his opponent. It seemed clear that at this point, Turook had figured out that somewhere another sphere existed in addition to the ones he possessed. And his search for it was in full force. No wonder Rimu looked worried.

I was told that I had been gone 36 hours from Tenaru. So I had been 36 hours in my own place and time (actually in my old truck), but I can't remember anything about it. It seemed to me that I hadn't left Tenaru at all; but finding myself a days walk from the village and hearing Rimu describe the events that happened while I was gone convinced me that my weird trip had really happened. I assumed that the "problem" Rimu had referred to in relation to my trip must have been related to Turook Tinboc's search for the sphere, but when I mentioned that to Rimu, he slowly pulled his attention from his sphere and focused his attention on me.

"Sit back down", said Rimu softly, as I paced his room in the cave. "I had hoped to have more information by the time we talked about this, but you must know at least what I can tell you now. There is quite a lot happening on several fronts at this moment, and much is interconnected. The unexpected scan by the green light, that I accurately predicted, indeed has to do with Tinboc's search for the orb. The reason I have been so unavailable to you these last few weeks is that I have known that Turook suspected the use of another orb. I have struggled to outsmart him and to prevent him from discovering proof for his suspicions, and to prevent him from finding the location of this orb. But I do not underestimate his craftiness or his intelligence. I had used the master orb to feed information to his three orbs, trying to trick Tinboc into believing he maintained the master orb in his possession. But he has always continued to suspect that one of "his" orbs was missing and being used. I mentioned to you that he is now regularly changing his search criteria and always searching for any use by an orb other than those he maintains. I believe that he has finally outsmarted me".

"Now, by Jove", continued Rimu, "our situation is most interesting!". "When you went back to your time, to allow for Thimlomarium to be cleared from your system, I felt it was necessary to send the orb back with you for two reasons that we can discuss at another time. I knew I could bring it back, but I would have to be without the orb for the time you were in transit, and I felt vulnerable in the absence of the orb while Turook Tinboc was so busy with his orbs. Still, I fooled myself into believing I remained several steps ahead of Tinboc. And I did not think he could find an orb 350 years in the past. I had planned for you to be gone for 24 hours, but when you were sent back, Turook must have detected and traced the energy of the orb. When I tried to bring you back after 24 hours, he was waiting. When I tried to activate the orb to return you here, Turook apparently attacked my orb with all three of his. All would have been lost if I had not had the master orb. But for the next 12 hours, we had to rely on instructions I programed into my orb prior to your trip to save your life. I'm only now learning what Turook Tinboc had his orbs attempt, but it seems that sever damage was done to you during your stay in your own time. The master orb was programmed to save you against attack, but to protect first your mind, then your physical body. Tinboc's orbs were instructed to put my orb into a continuous, repeating cycle, like putting a computer into a "loop", while his orbs found the purpose of my instructions and destroyed any ability to complete that purpose. The failsafe instructions in the master orb protected the ability to bring you back, protected your life, and resisted the other orbs. However, it took hours of time while the orbs battled before the master orb could open a window and escape from the attack of the other orbs, bringing you back. The energy of opposing orbs cannot even be imagined! We waited for you and the orb to return, not knowing at the time what was going on, but sure that it was not going to be good news. You were unconscious when you got back and the master orb indicated you had been badly damaged. I was terrified for you, but also terrified that Tenaru had been discovered as the location of the orb. Yet we brought you back a day's distance from the village and where no one lives, as part of a long-standing plan to confuse anyone trying to find this orb. You recovered and you seemed fine, but I was sure Tinboc knew an orb had been put "in play" by someone. I just hope he does not yet know who or where. That is why I thought a green line scan would undoubtedly be coming. And we only got back to the village just in time. Now Turook Tinboc will be searching with renewed effort, and Tenaru will certainly be suspect. The island will likely be searched, the level of Thimlomarium in our food may be increased, and I am scared to use the orb until I understand what Tinboc is doing. Now is when I need the people on this island free of Thimlomarium more than ever".

Rimu took a break for a drink and to quickly consult with the sphere he was holding, then continued, "Despite our problems, the orb is not wrong that you were damaged. When you again return to your time, I am afraid, no, I am sure, that you will find that you are not the same as when you left. I do not know how the damage will manifest itself yet, but you may be seriously injured. You are not damaged here because the orb was moving you and you were essentially taken apart at a molecular level when the attack occurred. The master orb cloned you and focused the attacking orbs on your clone that stayed in your time. As far as I can tell, there are now two of you, one in our time and one in your time. I will need to consult the orb before I can send you back to that time again for fear that you will meet yourself – a situation where the consequences are totally unknown. Unfortunately, you will not remember what happened during your transit or when you were damaged, and while you are in your time you will not remember anything about your time here on Tenaru. I am sorry. I have made rather a mess of your life. Indeed, it seems I have made a bit of a mess for the people of Tenaru. I'll let you know if I can learn more of your situation in your own time, but at this moment I must use the orb to prepare for whatever Tinboc might be planning. Forgive me, but I must get some sleep now, tomorrow will be a demanding day for me".

River and I made our way back to our hut in the village. I was still stunned from the information and implications of the day. I decided to take stock of my situation here; the food I had brought for the camping trip was essentially gone and I was now dependent on Tenaru to provide food (without Thimlomarium). I was in the middle of a political war, and technically in a political prison. The enemy was in name only, since I didn't know anything about Tinboc or his policies, but I had put my faith in Rimu and would help him if I could. The situation of the villagers was a life I would wish on no one. Thimlomarium! If only

Thimlomarium could be removed from the food, Rimu could have some help.

That thought reminded me that a couple of days ago Hanish had given me a sample of Thimlomarium-laced food. I found the sample in my hut on a box that served dual-purpose as a table. It was getting a little ripe, but the pea-green color was still unchanged. Water didn't affect the food, so what was needed was another solvent. I rummaged through my first-aid kit, then everything else I had left in the hut. My lab at Utopia University had probably twenty great choices of solvents – Benzene, Hexane, Toluene, DMSO, Ethanol, Chloroform, and dozens more. Here in the hut, I found three really poor substitutes for my experiment, a beer, a single-malt scotch, and a bottle of iodine solution. I split the contaminated food into six small piles and, after dumping out the fishing flies from my fly container, I put each sample in a separate compartment. I intended to do three duplicate experiments, using water as a control. The first extraction would compare beer versus water, the second would compare scotch verses water, and the third would compare the iodine solution versus water, each in duplicate. If I found anything that appeared to extract any of the Thimlomarium, I could repeat it using the water-extracted samples since I already knew water didn't extract or do anything to the effects of Thimlomarium.

The Iodine solution didn't do anything except turn the food red. After I removed the liquid to another compartment in the fly box and washed the now red food with water, the green color could still be seen in the food. The beer was also not very successful in extracting any significant amount of anything I could see, but it was a dark beer and the dark color seemed to overpower the light green of the Thimlomarium. But the scotch went from a clear/yellowish color to pea green. When I removed the liquid to a new compartment of the fly box, and washed the food with water, the food was left almost white. I repeated the experiment with scotch again with the same result. I dug in my pack and pulled out a hand-warmer and activated it by exposing it to air. Then I put the fly box on the hand warmer to see what would be left when the liquid evaporated. Some hours later, the scotch was the first liquid to evaporate leaving a light green powder coating the bottom of the compartment. I was pretty sure this was Thimlomarium, and if so, it could be removed by extracting with alcohol. Now all I would need would be gallons of alcohol and some "guinea pig" on which to test the extracted Thimlomarium.

Feeling that this might be my first real contribution to Rimu's community, I went out early the next morning to find Rimu. I came across Hanish in the village and, according to her, Rimu was off with the orb, and not expected to be back any time soon. So I explained to Hanish about the Thimlomarium extraction and asked if she knew where we could get a large quantity of alcohol. She had no idea what alcohol was and therefore I assumed there was none on the island except for my bottle of scotch. Damn, without sufficient alcohol, I had no solution to the Thimlomarium problem at all. I needed a "plan B". I could build a still, but had no metal for a boiler or condenser. The next worry was what could be fermented and distilled? I remembered that Hanish had served me a meal with a tiny amount for something like potato. That might be a good candidate for producing vodka, but there was not likely to be any large store of the potato-like things put away somewhere. Still, perhaps they could be grown this next season, and planting would begin soon. Unfortunately, the reality was that until we could extract the Thimlomarium, any food without it would need to be eaten, not converted into alcohol. Maybe there were wild grapes and I could distill a brandy. I asked Hanish if any fruit grew on the island, and used grapes and berries as an example. To my surprise, Hanish told me of the times her mother had brought back apples from across the forbidden pass. She said that beyond the pass was an old military base with a large apple orchard that had been carefully maintained until 15 years ago when Tenaru became a prison; since then the base and orchard had been abandoned. Hanish's mother had been one of only two people to cross the forbidden pass and return. How she had done it was lost when she died from the same illness that had almost killed Hanish. The only other person to cross the barrier had shortly after gone missing and was never seen again. Since his wife's death, Rimu had actively discouraged any trips to the pass area. The independence that Hanish had shown in going there had almost killed her too.

Yet, "There be apples!", and thus the possibility of making hard cider. To have a chance at getting rid of the Thimlomarium contaminating the food on Timaru seemed worth almost any effort. I asked Hanish if she could draw me a map to the forbidden pass area and tell me anything about it that would help me get there and back. Her answer was instantaneous, she simply said "No." However, she would personally take me to the pass, but she would not help me go alone. I didn't want to put Hanish in any danger, (particularly without Rimu knowing what we were doing) but we made a deal. Our deal was that we would go together so she would show me the way, but that we would explore only where we could safely; on the way there she would tell me what she knew of the pass and beyond.

I suggested that we wait until Rimu returned and let him know we were up to but Hanish dismissed that suggestion. It would take us until the late evening just to get there even if we left this morning and there was no sense in waiting. Moreover, she had traveled the island of Timaru alone since she was 20 years old and at this point knew the terrain even better than her Dad. There would be two of us so we could watch out for each other. And when we could figure out what we needed (if we got to or through the pass), we would come back to the village and stock up on men and whatever we needed, if we found anything. For now, we just needed to see if there were apples and if we could get to them. She said she would leave a note for Rimu so he would not worry about her. I had my doubts about how complete and accurate that note was going to be.

We agreed to meet in an hour by Rimu's cave and leave from there. I used the time packing a backpack with my gun, a hunting knife, first aid stuff, what food I had (three power bars and four instant oatmeal packets), River's food, water, clothes, a sleeping bag, and a backpacking tent. I also took a little of the scotch and the fly box, thinking that if we got to the apples, I would mix scotch and apple juice together on a small scale to make sure the acidity or some other component of the apple juice wouldn't inhibit the extraction of Thimlomarium by the alcohol. I could pick up another contaminated sample of food from Hanish before we left.

Fortunately, Hanish didn't run, but she sure could walk fast. We left the village an hour before noon and didn't stop walking until just before dark. We were traveling north, higher into the hills of Tenaru. The elevation rise was not excessive and so the walk was pleasant. The higher we went in the hills, the better I could comprehend the lay of the land for the island of Tenaru. I recalled Rimu once spoke of "no metal on this side of the island", and wondered how someone would block off an entire side of an island. But later I would learn that my idea of what he had said was a misconception. Along the way, Hanish filled in some history and what we might expect to run into. One thing we were sure to run into was an unhappy Rimu when we returned. Hanish admitted that had we let Rimu know where we were going before leaving, we would have had to accept a roadblock right off the bat. Her Mother had made this trip many times and had found a way past the "barrier"; a route she shared with no one else. Hanish had been with her a couple of times on the trip up the forbidden pass, but never allowed to go past the "barrier". On one of those trips, her Mother had acquired the fever that I had seen Hanish suffer from so badly. The Mother had died, and after that Rimu opposed any trips to this area.

The barrier, when we got there, would be a green line. This barrier would not be much different than the green line that scanned the island, but would consist of five pencil-thin lines at intervals from about 20 centimeters above the ground to a little over 3 meters. According to Hanish, her Mother had told her that if one did not touch the lines when crossing them, then one could walk freely on the other side. If you as much as grazed one of the lines in crossing, then you would be killed by a blast of energy on the far side of the barrier before advancing even 10 meters.  I should expect to see the bones and skulls of those who were lost in the teaching of that lesson.  If one made it past the green lines of the barrier, then it was only a few miles down to the peninsula where the old military base had been.  Unfortunately, Hanish knew nothing of the military site or the surroundings.  She had never seen the orchards, only heard of their existence from her Mother, but had eaten the fruit of these trees on several occasions.  She thought there might be a vantage point where we could see the area with the orchard, if we were willing to climb higher above the pass on steep rocky sidewalls.

The forbidden pass would turned out to be a relatively large valley between two canyon walls that narrowed at the summit of the pass.  One side was close to the ocean and appeared to drop precipitously into the ocean on the far side of that wall.  The landward side was equally as steep near the top.  But it looked like we could walk up the valley to the top of the pass with only moderate effort.  We chose to stay well below the pass to camp.  We would start early when there would be good light and spend the next day exploring along the barrier line and climbing up to find out if we could see the orchard.  The morning would be soon enough to meet the barrier.  I set up the tent and told Hanish to use it.  The weather seemed perfect in the evening and I had my sleeping bag, so sleeping under the stars seemed not just a do-able thing, rather actually a desirable thing.  We ate what little we had and turned-in as it got dark.

I awoke early to find the area socked in by a thin fog.  Actually, it seemed that a cloud had hung up right on the pass.  Unless the sun burned it off soon, this was going to screw up our ability to see anything.

To hell with it, I started my backpacking stove and heated water for instant coffee. I hadn't been drinking coffee since I got to Tenaru, initially worried about saving water. But now that was not a problem and I thought a shot of caffeine would do me good today. The smell awoke Hanish, and shortly she emerged from the tent with River beside her. Damn, I hadn't even noticed that River had slipped into the tent with Hanish. I had just assumed he was right beside me, guarding me. Seems she had made a friend. Hanish had never had coffee, but drank a cup despite not appearing to like the taste. I wondered what the effect of the caffeine would do to someone who had never experienced it, but anything that heightened our awareness this day would be a good thing, as long as it didn't give her a serious case of the jitters. Hanish suggested that we leave the tent up and plan to stay here again this evening after searching. We could leave anything we might not want to carry and hopefully cover more ground. Seemed like a reasonable idea to me, so I holstered my gun on my belt with my knife, took my first aid kit, some water and food, and a pair of binoculars, and put everything else in the tent and zipped it up. Today I would see the top of the forbidden pass and the green-line barrier.

In forty-five minutes, we stood at the top of the pass. The green lines were as obvious as traffic stop signs. I once had a buddy that could pole vault about 14 feet, but that was not a talent I had, and these lines looked to be as effective a barrier to me as a brick wall. We followed the lines east for a bit, but that side lead to a cliff dropping vertically to the ocean, so we retraced our steps and began looking west. This way also had vertical cliffs that curved around to the ocean, substantially further away. From where we stood, I could see that there was a peninsula below, maybe twenty square miles, surrounded by high impassible walls with only one access from the land – the forbidden pass. It wasn't necessary to have a barrier across the whole island, only across this pass, and only as far as the vertical walls on each side.

Hanish was wired! I don't think it had anything to do with the coffee, but rather her desire to get across the barrier. I explained again that crossing the barrier was not our intention today, just to explore and learn what we could that might help us find a way across. When she said she understood, I asked her to wait for me while I climbed a little higher on one of the cliff to see if I could get a look at the orchard and base below. When I returned fifteen minutes later, Hanish was gone. I would have seen her pass me if she had continued west, so I started walking east back toward the top of the pass. It only took a moment to find her. Hanish had found where a rock had rolled free (or been rolled free) of its resting place, directly under the lowest green line. The depression of the rock allowed Hanish just enough room to get most of her body under the green line – but not all of it. The V-shaped depression had allowed her to get her head and chest under the line, but not to come up on the other side without her hips and butt touching the line. She had worked at it so hard, she was now trapped and any movement she could make was likely to touch the line. It seemed funny to me at first, despite the fact that I was pissed, but it took only seconds to realize that she was actually terrified and really between a rock and hard place. I made her lie still and removed some dirt from around her using my knife as a spade. It was not quick going because about an inch down was solid rock ledge. After a while, I took hold of her feet, had her turn her head sideways and blow out all of the air in her lungs; then I slowly pulled her out from under the line. I got her out successfully, but it was a much more risky maneuver than I had any intention of attempting. It took almost 20 minutes to calm myself down enough to continue exploring. I swore to myself not to let her out of my sight again until we were back at the village.

We spent the morning and a good part of the afternoon walking the barrier line and examining the cliffs. Hanish found a route on one cliff wall that looked like a technical rock climb out beyond the green line that seemed almost possible. I thought that one time in my youth, when I was rock-climbing a lot, that I might have been foolish enough to try it. But Hanish was sure it was possible and assured me that she was an accomplished rock climber – trained by her mother. Regardless, I would not let her try it without ropes and safety considerations. No problem for Hanish, she let me know, she had rope in the bag she had brought and I could belay her. After her attempt to slide under the barrier, I didn't think this was a very good idea, but I eventually gave in once I was sure the rope would hold her. Hanish was like a ballet dancer on the face of that wall. She was careful, agile, and beautiful to watch as she moved like a spider across the rock. She was just clear of the green line when a handhold broke off and she fell. I caught her easily, but she banged into the jagged wall with pretty good force. I made her come back straight up, she climbing, with me supporting her by the rope in a manner to ensure she would avoid the green line. When she got back to where I was positioned, I could see she was bleeding from a cut on her arm. We wouldn't be trying that approach again. We walked back to a flat spot away from the green line, and I tended to her cut, which was still bleeding freely. I wiped it with an alcohol wipe, applied some antibiotic cream, and while I was wrapping the cut with gauze, I noticed a couple of rodent-looking critters following the blood drops on the ground. They would stop at each drop, lap it up and then move on to the next, getting ever closer to us.

They were kind of cute little guys, and struck me as something like a cross between a pica and a golden-mantel ground squirrel. But as they got closer, I could see that the real distinguishing feature of these animals was a set of canine teeth that looked like saber-toothed tiger fangs. These fangs were much thinner, like needles, and I wondered how they kept from breaking them. At first, there were two of the saber-toothed rodents. But, almost instantly, others began joining the first two critters; then there were suddenly four, then eight of them, each moving steadily closer to us. I tossed a rock and yelled. That caused them to scatter for maybe twenty seconds and then they regrouped, continuing to follow the blood trail toward Hanish. I threw a bigger rock and stood up yelling and waving my arms. This had the same effect, but for even a shorter time. By now, there were a dozen of the rodents and I was getting extremely uncomfortable about their persistence in closing in on us.

An idea struck me like a thunderbolt! Hanish had gotten her infection here; her mother had also gotten her infection here. Hanish had a cut on her leg when I gave her the antibiotics, and now I remembered the puncture marks below the cut. The infections didn't somehow just get into the wound, perhaps it was injected into her and her mother by these saber-toothed rodents. They were bloodsuckers. This location was perfect for them; anything that touched the green line was killed, and the collection of bones, human and non-human, on the other side of the pass testified to that. These guys burrowed or ran under the barrier. They got the blood for free.

So I wondered, were they drawn by, or to, blood? Did these critters harbor the infection that killed the folks of Tenaru? Another experiment was called for. I pulled out my gun and shot the closest saber-toothed rodent. My shot pretty much blew its head off (even though I was aiming for the center of the animal). I don't know which was more scared by the shot, the rodents or Hanish. Damn, I should have thought to warn her; this was getting to be a pretty stressful day for her. Oh well, she'd get over it. I ran over and picked up the dead rodent by the tail and let the blood drain into a depression in a rock. Then I tossed the remains of the rodent to the side. I took Hanish twenty meters back from the pool of blood in the rock and waited to see what would happen. Within minutes, there were over 20 rodents fighting to get to the blood. When the pool of blood was gone, they attacked the dead rodent's body. I was pretty sure my hunch about the saber-toothed rodents was correct.

We had seen most of what we needed to see and I wanted to think about how to get across the green line, so we headed back to camp. We would have no apples when we went back to the village, but I hoped by then I would have an idea of how to get across the forbidden pass. I suggested to Hanish that we climb back up to the pass first thing in the morning to try one more idea that was growing in my mind, and then make a "bee-line" for home.

That evening we talked about the pass, the green line and the rodents. We still had discovered no way across the barrier, but we re-lived the day to see if there was something that had happened that might give a clue we had overlooked. Reviewing Hanish's two close-call episodes got me a little hot under the collar; she could have been killed twice but for some luck and my help. I sure didn't need Rimu blaming me for the loss of his daughter, especially after the good will I had received for helping to save her earlier. But she laughed off my anger and thanked me for saving her once again. While I pride myself on being a scientist with decent observational skills, it was Hanish who brought to my attention that all the bones of things killed because of hitting the green line barrier were only on the far side of the pass. She had decided that it was probably safe to touch the green line if one did not pass through it to the far side. That suggested that only one side was protected, if her premise was correct. One could not go down the pass to the area of the old military base, but probably could leave from the base across the barrier with impunity. Equally dangerous was the potential to be bitten by a saber-toothed rodent. The consequences of a rodent bite were not as high tech as an energy blast, but without antibiotics led to same ultimate conclusion. No wonder this was a "forbidden" pass. There were at least two ways to get killed we now knew of, and possibly others unknown.

As the evening wore on, clouds began to appear on the pass again and the fog settled in. Hanish insisted I also sleep in the tent since the possibility of rain was increasing. It was too warm to be inside my sleeping bag, so I unzipped it and just put it over me. Hanish had a wool-like blanket pulled over a green plastic-like sheet of cloth material from which the coveralls the men all wore were made. By the time it was semi-dark, I was fast asleep. But I awoke in the night with a start. Hands were searching me, and when I tried to sit up, I was held down by strong arms. Just before fear set in, I recognized Hanish's voice saying my name and telling me quietly that everything was all right. "Al, Al…", she said softly, "Shhhh. It's alright, you don't have to say anything." The strong arms were hers. She let me go and when I started to ask what was the matter, she stopped me from speaking by covering my mouth with hers. When we came up for air, she put a finger on my lips and said, "Shhhh, three times I would be dead if it had not been for you. Now I am 35 years old and there are things I need to know and want to learn. There has never been a functional man on this island, except my Dad. Just help me because I'm new at this. You don't have to say anything". She kissed me again and let her hands explore. Thoughts and urges I had suppressed for 10 years came alive. I reached for her and found she was wearing nothing. We both learned and relearned. I think we were amazed at our stamina, and the night went by seemingly both slowly and quickly. In the morning we got dressed and made coffee together. We didn't say much, but our smiles told each of us what we wanted to know.

As we prepared to go back up to the summit of the pass one more time, I took the fly-fishing box from my backpack and put it in my pocket. I took one of the two syringe needles that I kept in my first aid kit and pocketed that as well. I strapped on my gun and knife and then took down the tent and repacked the backpack. Almost all the gear would stay here at our camp until we picked it up on the way back. Forty-five minutes later we were back on the ridge. I had picked up a hefty tree limb on the way up the pass in case the saber-toothed rodents tried to get too close.

My goal this morning was to see what effect Thimlomarium would have on the rodents. In one of the compartments of the fly box was the dried sample of Thimlomarium I had extracted with my Scotch whiskey. I added a little scotch to dissolve the chemical and when we got to the depression in the rock where I had drained the blood from the rodent I shot, I took the syringe needle and inserted it in a vein on my left arm. I let the blood run into the compartment with the Thimlomarium until the compartment was full. By now, the saber-toothed rodents were popping up their heads all around. I withdrew the needle and used it to stir the Thimlomarium in with the blood, then dumped the solution into the depression in the rock. By the time I got back to where Hanish was waiting, the first of the rodents was lapping up the blood. By the time the small pool of blood was gone, at least 30 rodents were trying to get their share. I had wondered what sort of concentration of Thimlomarium was needed to get an effect, and how long it might take to see any effect, if it occurred. I didn't need to wonder long; the effect was almost immediate. The rodents just sat where they were and refused to move. I tossed some rocks at them, but they ignored the rocks – even the rodents that had been struck by the stones. I slowly approached them with my stick, and when they still didn't move, I used the stick as a golf club and teed off about 25 rodents. Not one rodent moved before I launched it with my limb-shaped golf club off to the side of the trail up the pass. I was pretty sure that even if I didn't kill all of them with my stick, any rodent that had partaken of the Thimlomarium would fail to reproduce. We could use any Thimlomarium we would be able to extract to eliminate this particular rodent menace once and for all.

It was time to head back to the village. We stopped walking only one time for an hour. It wasn't to rest, but to satisfy our desires that had found full expression the night before. And we still made the village before dark.

# CHAPTER 9

## I should have retired

My standing in the educational community might have been significantly higher if I had not been in a position to ask certain questions in my past. I've always considered that I asked intelligent, even insightful, questions, and presented logical and concise arguments, but not everyone always agreed, particularly if I appeared to question one of their plans or their thinking. So, I was surprised to be asked by the school's President and the Provost to attend one of the largest and most prestigious of the educational pedagogy meeting in the country, to represent the University. It seems that, since I had been working with the University's Registrar to allow the College, of which I was the dean, to give credit for knowledge acquired elsewhere - based on a validation of that knowledge by testing - I was the logical person to attend this meeting. My boss wanted to determine the national mood of institutions of higher education on giving credit for courses not taught by the university awarding the credit.

Why would you want to give credit for something that your university did not teach? That seems, at first blush, to be dangerous to the reputation of a school; and many faculty members feel strongly that only they can provide or guarantee whatever level of quality is sought. However, there are some precedents for exactly this sort of credit being earned. First is the Advanced Placement (AP) exam. In many schools, students with successful AP exam results are allowed to progress to the next level of instruction with credit and without further prerequisites. Second, if a student can pass a College Level Exam Program (CLEP) test, in any of 33 disciplines, 2900 universities will award credit for the course. Currently, hundreds or thousands of online free courses are offered as Massive Online Open Courses (Moocs) by multiple institutions. A colleague of mine taught a math course as a "Mooc", with over 60,000 students in a single course. Although free of cost, they are mostly offered without credit for personal interest and advancement.

Now, I have always thought that knowledge is knowledge. If you have learned something, and (most importantly) can demonstrate that you know it, then you are educated in that particular area. So I had advocated for methods of validating learning, and allowing credit to be given for that knowledge, regardless of where it was obtained. There is a charge for taking the CLEP test, so why not allow a university (or College) to charge for a faculty-approved test to validate learning from Mooc courses, and award credit for validated, proven learning? This idea would be the proposal I would suggest at the national meeting I was to attend. We would see how such an idea might be received nationally.

The meeting venue was to be New Orleans. Great infrastructure, great food, and a warm climate in the winter timeframe of the meeting. My talk was to be on day two of a four day meeting; my plan was to stay around for a series of sessions and a plenary talk on day three, that were of interest to me, and catch a morning flight home on day four, since the last day was short on talks and long on business for the educational society that put on the meeting. Past experience had convinced me that meetings such as this were a great opportunity to visit with others having similar responsibilities and compare notes, as well as to reconnect with old colleagues and friends. I was pretty sure one of my best friends, who had worked at Utopia U for many years before moving on for a better salary, would be attending this meeting so I got in touch with him by email. It turned out that we would both arrive the same evening and we arranged to meet for a beer.

I met Jim in the hotel bar and the years we had been apart might never have happened judged by how easily we caught up on each other's lives and adventures. The stories were all funny, the beer went down too easy, and the hours too quickly slipped past my bedtime. We parted company agreeing that he was coming to my talk, I would go to his talk the morning of day three, and we would both go to lunch at a "local's" place of which Jim knew, before catching the plenary talk in the late afternoon following Jim's talk. Sounded like a good plan at the time.

Well, my talk went well enough, generating lots of questions and some promises to call me and continue the discussion. Jim's talk was even better. He presented a convincing pile of data clearly demonstrating that "problem-based learning" led to better understanding and longer retention than a standard lecture. Then, with the "working" part of our meeting obligation out of the way, we headed out for lunch at some greasy spoon restaurant Jim proclaimed to be famous for its red beans and rice. New Orleans red beans and rice is a local specialty with its origin in food the poor people could afford. This was not different from lobster in New England, but each dish had later developed into high cuisine, according to Jim.

I should have begun to get suspicious when I learned

that the only beers the restaurant offered were Bud Light and Pabst Blue Ribbon. As we walked in, a momentary view of the kitchen was enough to cause me to remember more than I wanted to about listeria, salmonella and other microbiological diseases. We got menus, but I decided it was safest to stick with whatever this place served the most. Jim and I each ordered the "famous" red beans and rice and a PBR beer to wash it down with. It turned out it took us three beers each and two hours to finish the red beans and rice served on a platter the size of a turkey carving board. We still had a couple of hours to kill before the plenary lecture we planned to attend and since we were so overfilled from lunch, we sat on the banks of the Mississippi river and swapped tails over yet another beer. About a half hour prior to heading for the conference venue, my intestines started to rumble. Jim seemed just fine, so I didn't say anything about it. Jim would tell me later that the same thing was happening to him, but he thought I was fine and therefore didn't mention it. By the time we wandered back, I had a case of gas that was going to prove embarrassing – I just didn't know how bad it was going to be.

We found seats in the middle-back part of the auditorium and waited for the talk to start. I soon noticed that I was not the only one with gas. Even when I wasn't the cause, there were still moments that could cause you to hold your breath. Jim seemed to have been affected as badly as I. The talk started and we tried to pay attention. But in our immediate area, concentration was decidedly interrupted on a regular basis by silent, deadly gas warfare. We are not talking about "Blazing Saddles" cowboy farts with lots of noise and duration. The clouds that surrounded Jim and me were silent, invisible and

unbearable. I noticed both Jim and I looking around as if
to see where the death clouds were coming from (as if we
didn't know). I was terrified that my rumbling intestine
noises were going to be heard over the speaker's voice.
The longer we sat there the worse the situation was getting;
soon there was little or no relief between the emissions of
both Jim and me. A few people finally got up and moved.
It seemed that everyone tried to ignore the fumes at first,
but with the first deserters to leave, the floodgates opened
and a full-blown (pun intended) migration began. That was
leaving Jim and me sitting in a circle of unoccupied chairs,
so of course we got up to move chairs as well.
Unfortunately, by splitting up we managed only to move
our trench warfare both further forward and further back
in the auditorium. This, of course, served to increase the
circle of unoccupied chairs, which was growing at an
alarming rate. The speaker could see what was happening,
but had no idea why. The middle back of the room was
emptying out and the sides of the auditorium were lined
with people standing along the walls or rushing out in
search of fresh air outside.

By the time Jim and I bailed and also went back
outside, for our own health, the middle back section of the
room was empty. I estimate we relocated over 150 folks;
but I was too embarrassed and in too big a hurry to get out
without being discovered, so I didn't bother to look for, or
count, any bodies that had passed out. I've always
wondered if the speaker during that lecture assumed that
the events that occurred were in reaction to his talk – I
hope he never knows better. But Jim does; he sent me an
Army surplus gas mask with a note saying it was for the
next time I have red beans and rice. I suspect the next time
will never happen, but I'm keeping the gas mask just in

case.

It should be no surprise that Jim and I agreed that we needed to stay outside as much as possible until we were normal again. Each hour and each trip to the bathroom seemed to be helping the situation, so we settled on going to a picnic on the shore of Lake Pontchartrain offered by one of the venders at the conference. It was a free dinner and outside, two good reasons in my mind. The draw for the picnic was a New Orleans crawfish boil. Being a Northwesterner, I had never eaten a crawfish. But I like shrimp so I figured it couldn't be too different.

There were lots of folks there and a sizable line at the table dishing out the crawfish. Jim and I picked up a preloaded paper bowl of crawfish, under some pressure from the line behind us not to hold up the line, and joined some other colleagues we knew from other universities. The conversation was great, but woo-who, the stew or chowder (what ever you call a crawfish boil) was spicy hot. The spicy taste made it difficult for me to tell what might be in the dish. Now, having a Ph.D. and years of teaching experience doesn't mean that at times one can't be as dumb as a bag of bricks. This was one of those times. I'm one of 1% of people who are allergic to garlic. As I was to learn, garlic oil is a key ingredient for boiling crawfish. But in my defense, I'd never had crawfish before and garlic didn't cross my mind. I don't have an anaphylactic reaction to garlic; I think (but don't know) that it lowers my blood pressure from a normally low level to close to zero. The one thing I do know is that if eat garlic, one second I will be standing and the next second I will be passed out. To make a long story short, after finishing the bowl of crawfish, I got up to get some water for some of us at our table, but on the way back I dropped over like a sack of potatoes, out cold. From what I'm told, Jim had dialed 911 by the time the water soaked into the grass. The EMT who loaded me into an ambulance checked for my pulse and could not find any pulse at all. He apparently didn't hold out a lot of hope for me.

Jim rode in the ambulance with me to the hospital. It was he who told me the story of my trip with the EMTs. First, the EMT who had checked my pulse called ahead to the hospital to alert them that he could hardly find a pulse and he thought that I would need to be put on the list for a heart transplant. I'm rather glad I didn't know that since I'm pretty attached to the heart I have. Second, he asked Jim what kind of work I did. When Jim replied that I was a dean at Utopia University, the EMT laughed and told Jim there was no need to worry about me then, since everyone knew that deans don't have a heart. Fortunately, I woke up a little before getting to the hospital. I explained that I suspected a garlic allergy, this sort of thing had happened before, and I'd be able to walk in 15 min, but I'd feel pretty bad for about 24 hours. I don't know if the EMT was relieved or disappointed. In any case, the hospital kept me over night, but released me just in time to check out of the hotel and catch my flight home. I had to call Jim on the phone to thank him. He loved the line about deans not having a heart and reminds me every time we talk. What bothers me is that I know he is telling the story to all of his students and has probably modified it with an emphasis that deans don't have a heart. I'm not sure if I'm bothered because the statement is correct or that it's not.

I don't have recurring episodes of passing out after eating garlic, but it takes 24 hours or more for the garlic effects to pass and for me to feel at all well. The flight back home found me not in a great mood and feeling like hammered excrement. I kept my phone in "airport" mode gratefully, but when I needed to change planes in Salt Lake City, I downloaded all new emails in case there was any new work related stuff. I was surprised to find an email on my personal email account from a friend in our Human Resources department. Since he was working at our university, he surely knew my work email address, and that I kept my work and personal email separate. That caught my attention and I read it first.

My HR friend asked me to meet him for lunch at a sandwich shop across town from the university as soon as I got back and not to mention this email to anyone. I interpreted that to mean that whatever this would be about was never going to be good news. Since it came to my personal email, I replied on my personal email that I would meet with him the following day at the shop he suggested. Damn, that only gave me less than a day to feel better and get my mind right for what was coming. I realized that I couldn't take too many more adventures like this conference trip had been. Now, completely exhausted, I would be entering the dragon's lair again tomorrow.

The sandwich shop was open but completely deserted when I entered. Not even a server was in the dinning room and I was looking forward to a cup of coffee while I waited. This was not a good sign for things to come. Five minutes later the server came in and apologized for not noticing me. My friend arrived in another five minutes, as I finished my first cup of coffee. We made small talk for just a couple of minutes when my friend pulled out a photocopied paper. He slid it over to me and explained that no one had talked to him about this paper, but he had found the original on the photocopy machine. After reading the paper, he copied it, and replaced the original in the machine. Five minutes later, the original was gone, picked up by the HR Director. From this point on, my friend would not admit to knowing anything about the paper or its contents, but we had been friends and there was something about the paper that didn't sit well with him. He asked me to do nothing at this point, which might give him away as the source, but to think about the implications and plan as necessary.

In summary, the paper was a memo from the University President to the Director of HR, informing him in confidence that I was to be fired or demoted. This directive was to remain confidential until I returned from my vacation (the camping trip I had planned over the anniversary of my wife's death) at which time the President was going to take vacation and, once he was off campus, the HR Director was to inform me that the President had lost confidence in me and I was to leave the dean's position. The reason was to be that I was not a team player and had disrupted the institution's efforts to build a new dorm.

I was dumbfounded, but now I could put the pieces together. I'd recently had a run-in with the Vice President for Advancement over a transfer of money from my college to the Advancement office for a new dorm. This VP was the President's "yes man", and had been kissing the President's ass for a decade. When I asked questions about the need for the money and the contributions from the other college deans, the Advancement VP was outraged and informed me the President would hear of this. He

didn't just talk to the President, he sent a letter to the
Board of Trustees calling me a disruptive, disrespectful
obstacle to the university. The fact that no other dean was
asked to contribute college funds wasn't mentioned.
Neither was the fact that I had told the VP of
Advancement and the President that if, in fact, they needed
the funds, that the President and VP for Finance had the
authority to move the funds without my approval.

I looked up from the photocopied memo and thanked
my friend. I let him know that I would wait to act until
after my upcoming vacation and would not do anything
regarding this until I got the memo from the President. No
one would ever know I had the information or from where
it had come. He said he needed to get back to work and
that he was sorry for the news he brought. I thanked him
again and told him that I'd explain the back-story to him at
a latter time. He left and I ordered another cup of coffee.

The money the VP for Advancement had wanted was
to come from a state and donor supported agriculture
project, but was going to be put into an account that was
hidden from the university system auditors. That's easy
enough to do if you hide it in a long-term construction
project, but it is unethical and I said as much at the time. I
had suggested that either the President or the VP for
Finance could transfer the money from the college account,
but it would have to happen without my participation.
Looking back on the situation, it seems even more
ominous now than it did then, most probably not legal. It
was also the beginning of the end for me; I could no longer
be counted on to give the President a carte blanche "yes"
without question. Therefore, it was time for me to be
replaced. It all reminded me of the removal of the previous

dean of my college, now it was my turn. I wondered what the President or Provost had wanted that the previous dean had refused.

It was getting under my skin that the President was going to fire me only after he left campus for vacation, so there would be no opportunity for me to talk with him personally. I don't enjoy conflict, but I have always considered it a responsibility to deal with people directly and in person. No one should be reprimanded or fired in "absentia". I now wish I had not given the President a towel in the bat incident.

I was a tenured professor as well as the dean, so getting rid of me from the university was going to be a difficult proposition. But administrators come and go at the pleasure of the President. I began to make a series of plans. Did I even want to be a dean working with a President I could no longer respect? Did I want to stay at Utopia U in light of the lack of moral backbone and an obvious preference by the President for "butt-kissers"? That evening, I filled a book with pros and cons for each potential decision. I decided in the end to fight the University, refuse to step down, and take my case to the university system and faculty union. I'd probably lose, however, I wanted to tell the President what I thought of him and his cronies to their faces.

But life is funny, I didn't have to do anything and I never got fired. After the end of my vacation, I was found in my truck and now I am on disability in an old folks home. Now, all I can do is type, lie in bed, and try unsuccessfully to tell my story. I never got the President's memo, there was no need to send it. I was replaced with an interim dean while folks wait for me to recover, but no one thinks that I will get better. In the two years I have been in the Alzheimer's unit of the Geezer Garage, the University President was investigated for unnamed irregularities and the university system's Chancellor summarily removed him from his position. The VP for Finance was allowed to retire and is now gone. The VP for Advancement moved to another institution that has all my sympathy for hiring him. And a new search is concluding for my successor as Dean. My son Jon told me all this, even though I doubt he thought I could comprehend what he was telling me.

One day I hope he gets a chance to read all this. I'd like him to know something about my work experiences as well as that I'm not a total vegetable. Sometimes the truth is stranger than fiction – yep, life is funny. It's enough to make anyone crazy. Did my last university President push me over the edge of sanity before he went? What, really, is the definition of crazy?

# Chapter 10

## New Directions

I met Rimu sometime near noon the day following our return from the forbidden pass. This time he came to see me. Rimu was obviously angry that Hanish and I had gone to the forbidden area and his knowledge of our events suggested that clearly Hanish had told him some of our adventures. I wondered just how much she had told him. But as we talked, he became less angry and more interested in the finding that Thimlomarium could be extracted from the food. Like his daughter, Rimu knew of no alcohol on the island and wondered aloud if the discovery of an extraction process would be of any practical use. We talked about other solvents with which we might try the extraction, but came up with no likely alternatives since the selection available on Tenaru was extremely limited. Fifteen years ago, before coming to Tenaru, alcohol had been readily available on the mainland where the Tinbock government reigned. But, for reasons now obvious, no alcohol had been sent to Tenaru, at least not in Rimu's memory.

My observation of the saber-toothed rodents, and my suspicion that they caused the deadly disease that had killed travellers to forbidden pass, proved to be of little interest to Rimu. His solution to that, and other problems associate with the pass, was to avoid going there. Although he knew from his wife about the apple orchard at the old navy base, the loss of the apples had seemed a small price to pay to reduce the number of deaths to the small number of residents (political prisoners) in his village. However, driven by the new possibility of making alcohol from the apples, we considered ways to get across the green-line barrier and whether materials might exist on Tenaru with which to make a still. Rimu's knowledge of the area was substantially less than that of his daughter and shortly the conversation turned to Rimu's activities while Hanish and I had been gone.

"Tinbock appears to currently be winning the war of the orbs, and it is becoming bloody difficult to protect those of us on Tenaru", offered Rimu. He then explained, "While you were at the pass, I took our orb some distance from here and risked using it. Indeed, in the last 36 hours I have slept only 5 hours and I suppose it shows in my disposition and thinking. It is my opinion that Turook Tinboc will not share his knowledge of the orbs he possesses with anyone, and he cannot share the existence of more than one orb since he has said that they were lost. Now, that leaves us in a one-on-one fight, with him verses me. I would say that I won the first few battles of our war, but he has now taken the offensive and seems to be winning. I have passively monitored his actions through our orb, and he has established a net or grid that is closing in on the location of any other orb that is used. I could, by not using our orb, slow the eventual discovery of our location, but we lose more than we gain if we just wait to see what Tinbock is doing. So I have instructed his Canalaska orb to spy on his Oceana orb and subtly alter a specific command. This operation will be leaked to him in short order, and will hopefully misdirect his search for the use of any orb not controlled by him. I may be able to buy us a little time, but only some number of weeks at the most. Indeed, using the orb yesterday may have given us away already, but I am hopeful that is not the case. In any case, our war grows more serious each day and our time for action grows shorter. I am considering some offensive actions from our side, but these actions would only give us away more quickly and on Tenaru we have so few people with an intact mind that we should be quite doomed, I think. Tinbock's retaliation will be quite severe. We might, however, get one surprise attack launched; but it had better be conclusively successful for we shall not have a second chance. Still, if we can remove only Tinbock, we will have removed the threat of the use of his orbs against us, since he is the only one who knows their control and their existence. Just know that before I initiate such a final battle, I will send you somewhere else, as you wish".

Rimu's anxiety was heartbreakingly clear. Something would have to be done soon to offer Tenaru some improved advantage in the conflict with Tinbock or the end was coming shortly. It was now only a matter of time.

That evening, River and I walked and thought about our situation (at least I thought about this situation, River probably thought of other things). Time was running out and there seemed to be very few options. My thoughts kept returning to alcohol, the apples, and the possibility that there would be materials at the navy base to make a still. I knew already that I was going back to the forbidden pass, and that I was going to try to get across the barrier, but this time it would be just River and me. Hanish would be pissed, but I would not subject her to the risk. As night settled in, I rummaged through the remains of what I had bought on my camping trip, looking for anything that might be useful. As I sorted the stuff, I revisited the conversations Hanish and I had about the pass, the barrier, and the rodents. The rodents were the least of the problems, they would be attracted by blood and that could be helpful. But the barrier was the real problem. I packed my backpack with the intent of staying for several days, cleaned my gun and got more ammo, and tidied up the hut just in case I didn't come back. Not knowing how long I would be gone, I decided to clean myself up as well. I took a sponge bath using my collapsible plastic bucket and got clean water for a shave. I could do without taking a razor if I shaved before leaving. But it was dark and I had a devil of a time shaving in the light of a flashlight until I repositioned the mirror to better align the light on my face.

Then it struck me! If I had three mirrors, I could probably get across the barrier at the forbidden pass. I knew immediately that I had two mirrors; one was the polished metal mirror that I always took camping and another was a small compact mirror I used to put in my contact lens. I would only need to find a third mirror. Yep, and people in Hell only needed to find ice water. But the solution was almost literally in front of my face. I have a green nylon bathroom bag that I use when I travel to keep all my toiletries in one place. I never take it camping, but this time had thrown it in my pile of stuff I was taking for no other reason than that it contained the only tube of lip balm I owned. It contains a small mirror sewn into the middle of the kit. I had never used it and didn't even realize a mirror was there, but the little mirror flashed bright as the flashlight beam swung across it. Thirty seconds later I had cut it free and now had three mirrors in my pockets and soaring hopes.

River and I left the next morning without a word to anyone. The villagers could not have cared less if I was gone. Rimu was preoccupied and Hanish had mentioned

that she was going to be involved in monitoring the orb. I
hoped I would have a couple of days before I was missed.
River and I made good time toward the forbidden pass,
partly because we now knew the way, but more
importantly, because I was getting in much better physical
shape.

That evening, once again I set up camp below the
summit of the pass, enjoying the memories of the last time
I had camped here with Hanish. But once the tent was set
up, River and I went up to the summit of the pass to do a
little work before going to sleep. I found some limbs of
appropriate length and sharpened them with my knife into
stakes. The mirrors were attached to the stakes with twine
at the top, middle and bottom of each mirror plate, leaving
room for shims at either the top or bottom to allow the
angle of the mirror to be adjusted. I picked a place along
the green line barrier, as far as possible from the largest
concentration of saber-toothed rodents that we had seen
on our last trip. With River keeping watch for the
approach of any rodents, I drove the stakes, to which I had
attached the mirrors, into the ground as far as they would
go and then put rocks around the stakes to stabilize them.
With the stakes as close to the green line barrier as possible,
I used my flashlight and shims, in the now late dusk, to set
the angle of each mirror to establish a light path that would
eventually redirect the lowest green line so that there would
be an inverted "V" in the lowest green line, leaving space
under the inverted "V" large enough to travel through
without touching the barrier line. I wanted the space below
the barrier to be as large as possible, large enough for
anything useful I might find at the old navy base to be
moved across the barrier, and so I set the farthest two
poles eight feet apart. Even with a middle pole and mirror,

relatively large objects could be manipulated, angled if necessary, and pushed underneath the barrier if one was careful. With the poles in place and the angles adjusted using the flashlight beam, River and I returned to our camp. In the morning we would finish the preparation and try to cross the barrier.

The sun rose bright and warm. I drank what I thought might be the last cup of coffee of my life, and then gathered my gear and headed for the pass. My thoughts were on the barrier. It would be no problem to see the green line in the daylight; the problem would be what happened when I pushed the mirrors into the barrier. When Hanish and I had discussed the barrier earlier, she had thought that touching the barrier was not enough to activate the killing blast of energy, but that something had to cross the barrier into the forbidden side to initiate the blast. That was supported by the presence of skeletons and skulls only on one side of the barrier, but wasn't sufficient to give me the confidence to test it with my body.

Another problem that River and I were going to face would be the presence of the saber-toothed rodents. They had not been a big problem the night before, but were sure to be out and about with the coming of morning. A pool of blood would buy us some time by keeping their attention, but maybe not enough time to cross the barrier and get out of their habitat zone. We would have to deal with the rodents first if we were to finish our preparations to cross the barrier.

We found our poles, with mirrors attached, undisturbed and standing adjacent to the green lines. Within minutes, the first of the rodents appeared to have noticed us and began a slow approach toward our position.

I held River back and prepared to shoot the closest of the rodents when they reached a certain point. Actually, when I did shoot, I shot two rodents. As before, the sound of the pistol firing sent the animals scurrying off for a short time. I used that time to gather the dead rodents, carry them to the depression in the rock that Hanish and I had used to create a blood pool, cut each throat, and drain the blood into the rock depression. Then, I carefully toted the two rodents, by the tail, back to our location at the mirror poles. Now working against a time limit set by the amount of blood in the pool, I prepared to push the mirrors into the barrier to redirect the barrier route.

First, I didn't know if the mirrors would redirect the green line or not, but since the green line that we hid from under the boat seemed to have the properties of light, it was worth a try. Second, I didn't know what would happen when the mirror touched the green barrier line, nor did I know if the mirror would continue to exist. Third, since I could only insert the mirrors one at a time into the barrier, the barrier was clearly going to register a breach until all the mirrors were in place, and what the breach would cause to happen was a large and dangerous unknown. Trying not to think about any of this, I grabbed the first pole and tilted it so the mirror (but not my hand) went into the lowest of the green lines. This reflected the green light upward, passing by the mirror on the middle pole, and clearly interrupting the continuity of the barrier. At the same time I moved the first mirror in place, I tossed one of the dead rodents through the barrier. Immediately, a beam of energy hit it while still in the air. I had no doubt that if the rodent had not been dead when I threw it, it would have been dead after being hit by the energy blast. Quickly I moved to the middle pole and tilted it into the beam, sending the beam back downward toward the third mirror. Again I threw a rodent through the barrier, and observed the same response as before. Now I tilted the third mirror to catch the barrier line and return it to its original course. I was rewarded with no new blast of energy, and the lowest level of the barrier could be seen to contain a perfect up-side-down, or inverted, "V" of green light.

River saved me from being bitten by the saber-toothed rodent. I was so intent on the barrier that I forget about the little bloodsuckers. A sharp bark and growl from the dog had caused the stealthy rodent to hesitate and gave me the time I needed to realize the problem, aim and shoot. Now a small pool of blood was forming near where River and I would need to cross the barrier, and a herd of rodents was quickly forming. Time had run out. I grabbed my pack and belly-crawled under the barrier, calling for River to do a crawl to join me. I was thinking about the rodents when I realized I was on the other side of the barrier and still alive. Clearly we had bypassed the barrier without touching the green lines and it appeared that we were now free to travel on the forbidden side. Sometimes, even a blind squirrel finds an acorn.

The peninsula appeared to be perhaps twenty square miles in size, but it was only about three miles from the pass to the old navy base. One half mile north of the path from the pass to the base was the orchard. The orchard was large and in reasonably decent shape for fifteen years without care, but the apples had all fallen and rotten on the ground. Spring was approaching in Tenaru and apples are a fall crop. I shouldn't have been surprised, but it had been fall when I had gone on my camping trip, and so the disappointment was crushing. Regardless, I continued on to the old base.  It wasn't a big base by my old Navy service standards, but may have housed 100 to 300 people.  As I wandered around, it seemed evident it had been hastily closed.  That would make sense if Tenaru had suddenly become a hiding place for dead civilization leaders and then a secret political prison.  One large ship was in a dry dock, in some state of disrepair, but not one sea worthy vessel was evident, either in the workshops or docks.  The original purpose of the base was likely for use as a repair base, since there were several large workshops, dry docks, crane facilities, and lots of tools.  Many of the buildings still contained their tools and machinery.  There was no shortage of metal on this part of the island.  Although I could think of nothing available that could be distilled into alcohol, without waiting until next year for new apples, I searched the base for components to make a still, regardless of the seeming futility.

One workshop contained a rack of 55-gallon barrels for oil or petrol.  If I could find some welding equipment, I might be able to use one of the barrels to make the boiler for my still.  In another warehouse was a gasoline-powered generator, and I made a mental note to remember it.  Yet another workspace was clearly a cleaning area.  There was a sandblaster, some large basins for washing, and a good bit of copper waterline that could be salvaged as a condensing coil for the now more and more probable still.  Also in that area was a large container of degreaser, and four 55-gallon barrels that appeared to be unlabeled, secured to a wall in a corner of the room.  The chain securing them to the wall had a padlock at one end, but it was not locked.  I freed the chain and rolled one of the barrels out for inspection, hoping to find out what was inside.  But no luck, I could find no writing on either the top or the side of the drum.  I was about to leave when River began smelling around the second of the barrels. I rolled it out so he could have access behind it; I didn't want to be surprised by a saber-toothed rodent again. But this time, underneath the dust on the far side of the drum was a different color. I used my sleeve to expose the writing. It read, ETOH/200. These drums contained 200-proof, pure, ethanol. No wonder they were chained to the wall, sailors the world over would drink this stuff, if given the chance, like it was party time. This was pure drinkable alcohol. Certainly the intended use was for cleaning some important mechanical or electrical components, but this was Tenaru's freedom from Thimlomarium in 55-gallon drums.

During a more complete investigation of this work area, I found an unopened five-gallon can of ethanol in a cabinet. The can went into my backpack and my attention went back to the village. I could extract enough Thimlomarium with 5 gallons of ethanol to eliminate all the rodents necessary, and the four 55-gallons barrels of alcohol could be used to eliminate Thimlomarium from the food supplies sent to the island. Rimu needed this information as soon as possible. And a lot of help was going to be needed to move over 200 gallons of ethanol to the village. Once more, I thought about that blind squirrel.

I made a very quick walk through the rest of the base and noted two rubber-tired carts. If the fifteen year-old tires would hold up, these might make the transport of the ethanol back to the village a lot easier than it otherwise would be if we had to manhandle those drums. But I was now in a hurry to get back home to share this fantastic find, so River and I started up the hill to the pass.

It was evening when we reached the pass. That

reduced the worry of the rodents, but meant that River and I might as well get some sleep rather than wander in the dark and use up my flashlight batteries. We found the inverted "V" in the barrier, still intact, and crawled under quickly. Hanish had postulated that we could simply walk out of the forbidden area, unmolested by the barrier, but now wasn't the time to do that experiment. Stopping at our earlier campsite, River and I spent an uneventful night and left for home at first light. By late afternoon we arrived at the village.

Rimu is a hard man to find, even in the best of times, and it was no different when we got back. I realized that would have to change; if we were engaging in a war, Rimu was going to be our Commander-in-Chief. Hanish would probably end up being a general, since she could lead the people of Tenaru with confidence. I was going to be perhaps a Lieutenant, or just a foot soldier. In any case, we would need quick and reliable communication, now more than ever. Regardless of what I perceived as a need, it took over two hours to find our Commander-in-Chief. But this time my news grabbed his full attention. Since Hanish would shortly be returning to their cave, he asked me to meet with him there in half an hour.

I scavenged some food for River, who was losing weight, and ate what food remained in my hut. I put away most of what was in my backpack, put on clean clothes, and headed for Rimu's cave, with River at my side. There was going to be a lot of work to be done, in a short time, to be able to extract the Thimlomarium from the food supply, but there was also going to be a need to consider how to go on the attack against Tinbock. This was going to be a long night.

Hope is a powerful force and it drove our discussions in the cave that night. Clearly, we had to do first things first, and most of the time was spent planning an expedition, including a large percentage of the folks in the village, to the old navy base to get the alcohol. The next day would have to be spent extracting Thimlomarium from food, using the five gallons of ethanol I had bought back with me. This would allow us to accumulate enough of the chemical to deal with the rodents at the pass, but would also allow us to begin freeing a select number of villagers from the effects of Thimlomarium. We decided to designate an area away from the village as the extraction site, to reduce the chance of contamination from the Thimlomarium we extracted inadvertently affecting villagers. Moreover, we would, as soon as we returned, build a longhouse and cook the food, from which we had extracted the chemical, in a central location. For the time being, we would control the food folks ate by preparing soups or stews for the entire village. Rimu and Hanish knew from experience how tired one could get of eating soups three times a day, but we would have little choice. Two hundred gallons of ethanol would go a long way toward creating Thimlomarium-free food, but it would be used up in short order if we didn't reclaim it. Therefore, when we returned to the navy base, it would be necessary for me to find the materials to build my still. Now we didn't need the still to create alcohol, but to redistill the alcohol, removing it from the extracted Thimlomarium, allowing the alcohol to be reused.

It took two days to prepare before we were ready to leave for the navy base. Rimu selected 20 villagers to accompany him, Hanish, River and me. Hanish suggested that Rimu stay at the village and monitor the pending war, but Rimu wanted to see the base and insisted that he could know what was happening since he was taking the orb with him. We would allow four days for the trip, but hoped to return with the alcohol at the end of day three. Rimu, Hanish, and I spent the day as we traveled to the pass discussing our plans to remove Thimlomarium and how to best wean the villagers off the compound. Unfortunately, none of us knew if there was a withdrawal effect. We decided to go totally Thimlomarium-free as soon as possible and watch for problems if they arose.

When we reached the pass, we armed all of the men with limbs to use as clubs against the rodents. The mirrors remained in place as indicated by the lowest green line still showing the inverted "V". I had dried the alcohol we used in the village to extract Thimlomarium, and prior to leaving had collected the chemical residue. Now it was time to make a cocktail of blood and Thimlomarium for the rodents. I deliberately cut my thumb and six or seven of the villagers did the same. We collected the blood and mixed it in with scotch-solubilized Thimlomarium. I distributed the mixture to five little bowls I had brought for that purpose, and set them out in a line for the rodents. Even as I moved back to the crowd of villagers, the rodents were moving toward the blood. I bandaged all the cut thumbs so we wouldn't leave a trail of blood, and we waited while the rodents consumed the blood meal. As before, the effect of the high concentration of Thimlomarium was almost instant. Soon, there were fifty rodents sitting by the little bowls. I clubbed the first few, but when there was no resistance on the part of the rodents, I let the villagers play golf with the remaining bloodsuckers. Shortly, there was not a living rodent in sight. Certainly there would be more rodents in the area, but there would be time later to repeat this process of eliminating rodents. We had just enough time to continue on to the navy base before dark. One by one, we all crawled under the barrier and walked without incident to the base to set up a camp in one of the barracks buildings.

The next morning, River and I showed Rimu and Hanish around the base. We found the rubber-tired carts and constructed ramps so the villagers could roll the barrels of alcohol up onto them. We were able to put three barrels on one cart, and secure them with the chain that had held them to the workshop wall. The second cart, therefore, only needed to carry one alcohol drum and had sufficient room remaining for the parts I needed for building a still. The rest of the day we looked for other useful items at the navy base and I worked on parts of the still. Hanish found a kilogram of salt in a cupboard, but there was no food left at the base. After 15 years, I'd have been afraid of any canned food anyway.

While we stood on one of the docks, Rimu pointed out into the water to show Hanish and me the location of the closest point of the mainland to the island of Tenaru. We couldn't see the land, but Rimu was confident that about ten kilometers away (six miles) was Invercargo, the town containing the headquarters of Tinboc's government.

We spent another night in the barracks but still didn't begin our trip back the next day mostly because I hadn't found all the materials I needed to complete a still. It turned out to be a bigger job than I thought to get the amount of copper waterline I wanted. But eventually I found what I thought would be sufficient resources, finished constructing the parts, and we loaded the second cart. We could have left in the late afternoon, but we would need to unload the carts to cross under the barrier, and reload to continue our trip. So we decided to wait until the next morning. I think Rimu got the best sleep he had experienced in weeks. The next morning, six people were assigned to push each cart. With Hanish and me taking shifts, we were able to rotate 3 or 4 of the team members each hour so everyone got a break from pushing. The trip was exhausting, but relatively uneventful and we successfully got our load back to the village at nightfall on the fourth day of the trip.

All the way back to the village, even while I pushed the cart, I spent my time thinking about how to take the battle of the orbs to Tinboc on the mainland.

# Chapter 11

## Out of my mind

The green glow of the digital clock in my room at the geezer garage said 4:07 am when I woke up. My mind was racing and my body felt tired. Tired from what? I don't do anything but sit up and lie down. There were four hours before anyone was going to set me up at the computer table; and those would be long, hard hours to wait. I only had one thing on my mind today; I was back in my "right" mind and aware that I was responding to my own thoughts. I also knew that I must have spent some time in my "other" mind (which I now think of as the Tenaru story) since the geezer garage room decorations had been changed without my notice, and the calendar date was long past (weeks) from what I remembered. I wonder if this is what Alzheimer's disease is like? Long periods of time missing and no ability to hold onto any thoughts from that time.

But I was also sure that there would be a new Tenaru story for me to read on my computer. I was especially interested because now that I was in touch with my brain, and I wondered if I could find any links between the "me" that I know and the Al Hart in the Tenaru story. I've been assuming for a couple of years that there really was no link, and the time my mind was effectively "gone" and out of my control was just a dream or a crazy man's illusion. Recently, I am wondering more and more about what is real.

Over the period of a couple of days, I typed almost nothing, but read the newest installment of the Tenaru story. Then I reread all of the Tenau stories that I have typed from the beginning (when I was found in my truck). Then I read it all again and made mental notes to link the miserable life I have in the geezer garage to the amazing adventure I read that I am having on Tenaru. This must be the definition of crazy: when one tries to link a dream or hallucination from one improbable time and place to events in the real world. But the only thing I seem to have is time.

Here is the list of things that I want to consider:

1. I was moved to a new place and another time by an orb or sphere.
2. All of my backpacking gear from my vacation is in the Tenaru story intact.
3. Time zones and seasons seem to have changed appropriately for the supposed move.
4. River had exactly the same amount of food from the camping trip when we arrive on Tenaru.
5. River doesn't know where we are on Tenaru, but knows all the commands I use.
6. My boat makes the trip with no changes.
7. The number of beers and kind of scotch I have in Tenaru are exactly the same as I took on the camping trip.
8. I get sent back to my truck, near Marble Creek.
9. An orb war on Tenau creates a battle on earth that leaves me damaged.
10. I'm found in my truck immobile.
11. The length of time I write about in Tenaru correlates well with the time I don't have control of my mind.

12. I can only remember 24-48 hours at a time in the geezer garage, when I have control of my mind, a time equal to clearing Thimlomarium from my system.
13. I remember nothing about events on Tenaru when I'm here in the geezer garage, but Rimu has offered an explanation for that.
14. When I read about the choices I made in Tenaru, they seem like the decisions I would make when in control of my mind.
15. Rimu says he can send me back to my time and place.
16. Tenaru is a lot more interesting than here.

So what seems more likely or real? Did I get transported to another time and place where I'm still a whole person? Did I go crazy and my brains connections are all screwed up? Do I have some dementia and my mind works differently now (or not so well)? Did I have a stroke that "blew up" my brain and it is now doing its own thing independent of me?

The fact that I even considered transport to another time and place in the list seems like pretty good evidence that I'm crazy. But why do I have to read about the Tenaru story, why can't I remember any of it? Why do I feel anxious in the geezer garage after something exciting or strenuous has happened in the Tenaru story? Can my mind produce a fictional set of stimuli so complete as to fool me that I am living a fantasy life and believing that it is real?

If I'm crazy, then I have lots of reasons why I could accept that to be the case. My time at the university, all those crazy weird stories of bosses and colleagues, would be enough to drive anyone over the edge. But I don't feel crazy. When I control my mind in the geezer garage, I think like I'm use to doing, and feel like I can reason well enough. When I don't have control of my mind (in the Tenaru story), the things I read about are not unlike what I might have done in a similar situation here in Idaho. All in all, it doesn't feel crazy. If my mind is doing its own thing, out of my control, then I have come to the conclusion that I like the Tenaru story better than I like my "real life" situation in the geezer garage, and I would chose to be in that story over the one I assume to be real. Unfortunately, the choice does not seem to be mine, at least not mine to make from the geezer garage, since I have no control over the events in the Tenaru story.

If somehow, I can slip permanently into the Tenaru story, either in reality or just in my mind, what happens to my life here? What happens to my son, Jon? Without the ability to communicate, I'm not much use to him anyway. Do I just die and that's the end of the story, or do I live on in my mind as long as I draw breath here in the garage, or is there another time and place where I'm living independent of my life in the geezer garage? At the moment, in my mind, any of these possibilities are just as reasonable as any other.

At this point, they are coming to take me from the computer and put me to bed. I guess I'll just have to let my thoughts incubate and write more tomorrow. Unless the time for me to control my mind is up.

# Chapter 12

## Time and time again

As before, I woke up with Rimu waiting for me. I was once again a full days walk from the village. I had to be told that I had been sent back to my time to clear the Thimlomarium from my body. That was more complicated now, because I had to take the place of the damaged body so I would not accidently meet myself. How and where Rimu moved the damaged body that was in my time, I don't know. Moreoer, Rimu had to activate all the orbs at once to defeat the pattern that Tinboc was using to search for orb use. That gave away that there was another orb controller beside Tinboc, but not who or where. I remembered nothing of going anywhere. But Rimu used the time marching and jogging back to the village to fill me in on what I missed while I was gone. I remembered the trip to the old navy base and the collection of the alcohol, as well as my thoughts on challenging Tinboc, but some amount of time had passed and I was clearly behind in my knowledge of recent events.

Rimu, Hanish and I (with River), met again in the cave to discuss our options with respect to preparing Thimlomarium-free food and the status of the battle with Tinboc. Although I had spent a whole day, on the way back from the navy base, thinking about taking the battle to the mainland, Rimu had evidently spent a year, or years on that subject. The discussion of food took little time, although we wondered how long it would take, on clean food, for an individual to regain their faculties. Rimu thought perhaps only a week or two, if we could avoid low levels of the chemical contaminating people. The war, on the other hand, dominated our discussion for a long time.

"Here is what I know at the moment", said Rimu. "I have never gone back to the mainland because I would easily be recognized by many people. I have felt that my safety resided mainly in the fact that I was considered 'officially' dead. But time has almost run out for us on Tenaru, which is especially sad since we now have hope of being free of the curse of Thimlomarium. Turook Tinboc has just now refined a worldwide net that will detect the use of energy from any orb, as a result of your last trip back to your time. Therefore, I am hesitant to use ours unless it is absolutely necessary, though I can use it passively as a monitor without giving off energy. Still, that gives Tinboc the advantage and relegates us to trying only to play defense to his initiatives".

"As with many dictators, Tinboc is not supported by a vast majority of the people, but all are afraid of him. Until his power is eliminated, we cannot expect the help of common citizens from Oceana. But our biggest problem is his ability to protect himself by using the orbs. He does not need to be holding one to make it work for him. He keeps an invisible field of power around him at all times; I suspect it is just the size and shape of his body, but the protection against any outside attack is complete. With my orb, I can do the same for myself, or us. But I fear a protective field weakens as it is made larger. So putting a protective field around Tenaru would likely both get us detected and produce a weaker field than Tinboc's field. This is all speculation, of course. However, in the last few weeks, I have experimented with making fields and merging them. This almost got us detected by Tinboc, and certainly caused him to create the net to locate orb energy".

"I think the alien energy beings, that gave us the orbs, used them for space travel and allowed the fields to be merged so they could be together and protected at the same time. If this is so, then the only thing Tinboc has to fear is another orb's protective field merging with his. I hope, with every fiber of my being that he does not know this, since he has thought he had all the orbs he might not have thought he could be challenged by another orb. I have been thinking that, as a last resort, I will visit Turook Tinboc, merge my protective field with his, and hope to surprise him sufficiently to take his orb or orbs. Of course, if the merger does not work, then all will bloody well be lost".

Hanish was adamant that Rimu not try this approach, and I found myself coming to her aid in the argument. "Let's consider the element of surprise", I interrupted, "surprise and the hope that Tinboc doesn't know that fields can be merged are our best weapons at the moment. But you have said that you will easily be recognized. If Tinboc recognizes you, he will certainly be put on guard for anything you might try. Moreover, Tinboc is younger than you and likely stronger. If he is aware of any danger prior to the meager of the fields, he'll be ready to overpower you without the orbs power, or ready and prepared to use the orbs power to stop you. Each of these factors makes your chance of success less likely. The plan you suggest is fine, but you can't be the one to do it since you are too recognizable".

We discussed Hanish making the attempt, since she knew how to control an orb, but Tinboc would certainly investigate who she was (and probably find out) before giving her an audience. I was the logical choice. I had in my favor that I had a distinct accent from another time, I could not be traced by Tinboc's people, Tinboc would certainly see me if I told him I was from a time near the events of McMurdoc's Folly (and had a dog with me) and mentioned an orb or sphere, and there was no *a priori* reason for me to be a specific threat to him as a stranger that had just appear out of nowhere. The down sides were that I didn't know anything about orbs, putting a field around me would require Rimu using the orb, and I still had to get to the mainland without being detected or giving away the location of Rimu's orb.

Rimu began to pace in the large room of the cave; "Such an undertaking is extremely dangerous", he spoke softly. "I can activate a protective field around you when you are on the mainland, just before you meet Tinboc. Perhaps it will come too late for him to notice, but in any case, he will not immediately know where the power came from since the effect will happen in the vicinity of all of his orbs. He is not a trusting person, and while he will be on guard, the off-hand mention of an orb will get his attention and he will want to speak to you privately to see what you know and if you know about his other orbs. Clearly, he will not allow you to touch him, not even to shake hands, so I will have to expand your protective field to perhaps a three-meter diameter so that the fields will merge. He may or may not know that a merger has happened. But you will need to be as close to him as you can get. If he has an orb with him, you must get it from him before he can even think of using it. Then Hanish and I will try to keep his thoughts from the orb. He does not need to hold an orb to use it; remember this, whether or not he is holding an orb when you meet him, you must kill him or render him unconscious immediately when the fields are merged. With a protective field around you, only Tinboc can harm you, but he will kill you without hesitation. And you must not leave an orb to be found by others. We still have the problem of getting you to the mainland without the orb giving away our location when you are sent".

"I'll manage that part", I explained to Rimu, "the carts we brought the alcohol back with are made of wood and I think we can convert them into a raft. With the wheels removed and the axles on the top, I can mount my boat as a cover and not be seen or counted by a green-line scan. If you have enough of the green cloth everyone wears, we can do a little sewing and I'll set up a gaff-rigged sail on the raft without much problem. I can sail at night and take down the sail and row in, using my boats oars, once I get close to the mainland".

Now it was Hanish's turn to suggest what the rest of us had overlooked. "Do you think", she questioned, "that Al can find the town, or the government buildings without bringing attention to him too early? He will need a guide, and since you can't do it, Dad, I will go with him. I have seen your maps of the area and the layout of the buildings, so I can get him there".

"What if something goes wrong, how will you get back?"

"I won't, at least not immediately, but that will be a small problem if the plan fails. In fact, I may be better off not being on Tenaru".

Rimu spoke only one word, "True".

Since the old navy base was the closest point to the

mainland, it looked like we would have to make another trip back there. Actually, I was getting a little tired of giving up my blood to the blood-sucking rodents, but we'd cross that bridge when we got to it. First, the extraction of Thimlomarium from the food had to be achieved on everything that was to be eaten. Drying the alcohol gave us a good supply of the chemical, but it meant that we lost the alcohol. We needed to re-distill and reclaim the alcohol. I could finish the still in a couple of days so that became my immediate project. Rimu and Hanish went over maps and plotted how to get us into Tinboc's presence. Their work seemed much more important than what I was doing.

We refined the extraction process and in a couple of days were ready to try the still. I showed Rimu how to use it; he could teach others. Then we developed a soup line for cooking and serving. Regardless of our success on the mainland, the folks on Tenaru would be able to free themselves of Thimlomarium and, with luck, return to the functional people they use to be, folks who could help Rimu run the village. Still, if our plan to take the battle to Tinboc was not successful, these were going to be really skinny, hungry people if they had to exist for long on only what food could be extracted. But with spring coming, it would soon be time to plant new crops and hopefully the people on Tenaru would live long enough to benefit from a bountiful harvest. If only Tinboc didn't find the orb on Tenaru first.

Other than a nagging fear in the pit of my stomach, there was no further reason to postpone the trip to see Tinboc. Hanish didn't show the slightest concern; which is more than I can say for myself. We got six villagers to accompany Hanish, River and me back to the pass. We took both carts with us, one loaded with my metal boat. My little boat would have gotten us to the mainland faster than a raft, but we needed the metal cover to protect against a green-line scan. Once we got the carts and boat to the old navy base, Hanish would take the villagers back to the pass, make sure they got safely across the barrier, and send them home. The two trips over the pass took blood from all six villagers, Hanish, and me to keep the saber-toothed rodents at bay, but there already seemed to be less of them.

Now there were only three of us, counting River. I worked on constructing the rafts and rigging a sail. Hanish used the time to instruct me on the plan to get to Tinbok, and to give me a more detailed history of the father and son Tinboc administration. We discussed what to do with Tinboc if we were able to capture him. That probably should have been funny, since we would then have the lion by the tail in the middle of its lair. Somehow, we never got around to what we might do if Tinboc got the best of us. There was an assumption that if he found out who either of us were, we'd not be alive to worry about it for long. I intended to meet with Tinboc alone; Hanish intended to be there with me. It seemed best to avoid an argument now, and I'd figure out how to get to Tinboc alone at a later time.

Hanish had some way of alerting Rimu when we were ready to set sail; it was likely that he was continuously monitoring her. We left Tenaru at full dark, I was pretty sure we could keep a pretty straight course using the stars as long as the sky was clear. I wanted enough light to be able to see when we got to the mainland. It turned out to be a warm and clear night, but the wind was low for the first hour, still the three of us moved slowly away from shore. Well before midnight the wind freshened and we sailed at a slow but steady pace that suggested we would cross the six miles to the mainland easily before dawn. I took us most of the way straight toward the mainland, but then angled to the east. I hoped to be close to the mainland shore by the time it was daylight, but wanted to be in a low population area. We would drop the sail when it was light to lessen our chance of being seen. So I didn't want to be too far eastward, but likewise, I didn't want to crash into the shore in the dark. We could land and walk back westward, or use the metal boat and row, but each option had its own risk. The better solution would be to sail our way back toward Invercargo just as dawn was starting to break.

I was amazed that the jury-rigged raft and sail worked so well. We actually sailed up to the mainland shore and were within two miles of town. We did a lousy job of hiding the raft, but tied it up securely so it would be there if we needed it. In the back of both of our minds was the thought that if we succeeded, then Rimu could use the orb to bring us back to Tenaru, and if we failed then we wouldn't be needing the raft at all. Still, it was some small comfort to know that if we couldn't find Tinboc and nothing came of our trip, there was a ride home.

My worries increased the closer we walked toward the town. My clothes were unusual here to say the least. But Hanish looked perhaps even less in style. It was decided that she could not show up on the mainland in the green cloth that all the people of Tenaru wore. So she modified a pair of my nylon hiking pants that had started out way too big for her and she had on a blue work shirt of mine with the sleeves rolled up. I found it really attractive on her, but I had been assured that we would not look like other mainlanders. Hanish would do all the talking until we were able to speak with Tinboc, and then I would do the talking with him and just let Tinboc assume that Hanish had come with me from the past. I wanted to have him invite me into his office, where he would think he could kill me without observers if he felt the need, to have a conversation about the orbs I was going to mention. That would keep Hanish out of harms way, at least initially. If something happened to me, hopefully Rimu would see and could let Hanish know to get the hell out of town.

It was correct that we were dressed unlike the people we met. The dress here was closer to a long dark kilt for both sexes, worn with a very shinny waist-length loose-fitting white blouse. But I hadn't need to worry about our dress, those we met hardly saw either of us; no one could get there eyes off of River. A dog was not something people here had seen in over two hundred years. Some folks were terrified, others were just interested, and others had no idea there was any danger and just wanted to touch the strange thing. I had even greater admiration for Rimu, who had known immediately that River was a dog, but I knew by now that he was indeed a serious historian. Not surprisingly, word of our arrival got to town before us. As Hanish led us to the government building, we were met by about a half dozen police and a low-level government official. This was going to be a major test of our ability to get to Tinboc; I had my loaded pistol tucked into my belt at my back (the holster would have been too obvious) with my shirt outside my pants to cover it, a fully loaded extra magazine in my coat pocket, and my knife in a green cloth pocket inside my boot. If these were found, I was sure my reception would not be as welcoming as I would have hoped. Hanish also had an over-the-shoulder bag with God knows what dangerous stuff in it. She never failed to amaze me, so I was pretty sure she had some plans for her own protection. I was also sure I wouldn't want to be on the receiving end of her plans if she felt threatened. But anything we had was child's play compared to the power of an orb.

The greeting party stopped us and asked unconvincingly if they could help us. Again, River was the star of the show. Having him with us was like walking through New York City with a live T-Rex. None of the party was sure what River was; but his good behavior seemed to work to our favor. Hanish said we had information about an orb from a former time and we would need to talk with the head of the government. Cleverly, she did not use Tinboc's name, and left everyone wanting more information. But she insisted we would talk only to the head of the government, and our time was limited.

Probably because we had the equivalent of a T-Rex with us, we were led into the government building with three of the police in front, and three in back of us. We were put in a waiting room and the government official brought us something like coffee. This was clearly an action to delay us so that our images from the multiple security cameras could be reviewed and our identities determined. After our second cup of faux coffee, it seemed that we might have proven difficult to identify. Hanish caught the government employee and simply told him that if the government did not want the information on the orb, we would be leaving. The official protested

and tried to physically restrain Hanish, by escorting her to
her seat. Without a word from me, River was at Hanish's
side, growling and baring his teeth. The government man
pulled his hands back like Hanish was red hot, and he went
white as a ghost. I'd never seen River do that for anyone
but me, but when Hanish reached down and petted him, I
could see there was a real attachment between those two.
What? Was that treason from my dog? But I had to admit
I like her too and River was a smart animal. In any case,
the government man couldn't go off to find Tinboc quickly
enough. Even the police gave us a little more room.

Within ten minutes a well-dressed man entered the
room. He introduced himself as Turook Tinboc, the Prime
Minister of Oceana. Hanish recognized him, but gave
almost no indication. I would not even have known him if
he had not introduced himself. He was shorter than I was,
probably twenty-five pounds lighter, but in pretty good
shape and carrying no extra weight. I was glad that Rimu
had been making me run all over Tenaru, helping me to get
in shape, and especially glad the Rimu had not tried to take
on Tinboc himself. Now it was my turn. I nodded to
Hanish and bowed to Tinboc. I explained in my accented
English, that I was from a time near McMurdock's folly
and had information about the orbs, but I must speak to
him in private. When I used the plural form for the orbs, I
could see a shocked response. He really didn't want
anything said about orbs in a public setting. He invited me,
alone, to go with him to his office. I think he was
chauvinistic enough that he considered Hanish less
important, fulfilling a thought on which I had been afraid
to pin too much hope. Hanish turned bright red when
River and I started to follow Tinboc, but she didn't say
anything. Tinboc stopped short and spun, pointing to

River.

"I said you alone".

" I go nowhere without this animal", I replied as I turned and started walking back to Hanish. "Let's go", I said to Hanish.

As she stood, Tinboc raised his hands and said, "Alright, you can bring it".

We followed him to the same office Rimu had described, although it was probably much more secure now than when Rimu had been in it fifteen years before. I had River sit and that seemed to please Tinboc. As Tinboc went to his desk, I gave River a very soft command of 'at the ready'. River was now a charged weapon waiting for a command to attack.

Tinboc wasted no time. He began, "I'm a very busy man, what do you know about the orb? They were not even known to mankind in the time of McMurdock's Folly".

"Not orb, but orbs", I said. "You know they cannot be destroyed. The orbs must be used as the aliens intended; I'm here to tell you that hoarding the orbs will not be allowed".

"But there is only one orb, only the Oceana orb, the others were lost at sea years ago. Perhaps they will be found one day. This must be the one you are talking about", said Tinboc, pulling an orb from his desk.

Now I was really scared, he was holding the orb and a thought could probably kill me. But I was hoping that Rimu had activated the field around me and was about to merge the fields.

"May I look into it", I asked. " I won't come close enough to touch it and you have mental control. I just want to verify which one it is". Again I caught Tinbock by surprise. The real surprise was that I was totally faking it.

" Certainly", he replied, "but please come no closer than the front of the desk".

As I went to the desk, the office door burst open and a policeman dragged Hanish into sight.

"Prime Minister, we have identified her and it is important you know the identity"!

"So tell me, quickly", said Tinboc standing.

At that time a voice came into my mind. It was Rimu's voice. "Now! Do it now. The fields are merged".

"Attack!" I called to River. "Get the ball".

Before the policeman could answer Tinboc and before Tinboc could take his focus from the policeman, River had Tinboc by the wrist and had shaken the orb free of his grip. I knew Tinboc didn't need to be holding the orb to use it, and that River was going to be the target. The rest happened at the speed of lightning and by reflex action. I pulled my gun and shot Tinboc twice. His eyes went wide as I surprised him one last time, since he felt secure within his field. I doubt he even knew our fields had been merged. As he slid down the wall behind his desk, I took careful aim and shot a third time into his brain. I wasn't going to give him a chance to recover from the initial shock and activate the orb. I had never shot a man before, but now I had deliberately killed a man I had only just met.

But this wasn't the time to worry about that. I spun to point my gun at the policeman that was holding Hanish. But he too was sliding toward the floor with his throat cut and a knife sticking out of his chest. Hanish was more interested in seeing if Tinboc was really dead than she was about the any threat from the policeman.

I quickly shut and locked the office door. "Hanish, can you get word to your Dad"?

"Yes, what do you want to say"?

"People will consider that Tinboc has been assassinated and it would be best if everyone thinks it was done by someone from the past. Tell Rimu that once we have Tinboc's orb, to put you and River and me all inside the energy field. We are going to walk out of here telling everyone we meet that we are from the past and that Tinboc disappointed the aliens by his use of the orb. When we are out of the building, Rimu can use his orb to bring us back to Tenaru. The fact that we will just disappear will be good for the story. If we have the only orb that is out of Tinboc's office safe, then the others are secure until Rimu can figure out how to open the double safe. But unless Tinboc has been training someone to use the orbs, something Rimu doubts, then Rimu is safe to use his orb to bring us back".

Walking out of that building with my arm around Hanish was really fun. The police tried to stop us. They didn't have any guns, but used batons, some kind of electrical device like a Tazer, and a field that created a cage, but none of them had any effect against the field Rimu had put around us. I told them, in my best old English, we had done what we had been sent to do, we would not hold their actions against those who tried to restrain us, but that we were done now and going back to our time, so they should save their efforts and adhere to what had been taught on Instruction Day. Moments later there was the familiar blinding white light and we were on Tenaru right next to the village. Whatever might happen in the future, it was now going to be a fair fight. Tenaru now had two orbs and the other two were locked, at least temporarily, in an unknown safe in Tinboc's office.

With a little digging through my stuff, I found some treats for River and gave him the praise he deserved. I suspect Hanish did the same when I wasn't watching. She was going to be a real threat to me for River's affection, messing with my best friend. Stupid dog was love struck.

Finally, Tenaru was going to get the chance to free itself of Thimlomarium and possibly from being a political prison. None of us missed the implication, that without the threat from Tinboc, Tenaru could shortly send people to the mainland for non-contaminated food, and that even the extraction of Thimlomarium might not be necessary soon.

There were only three of us, at present, able to celebrate the success of our battle with Tinboc. Rimu, Hanish and I sat in the cave and talked about the future. Rimu postulated a short period of chaos in the government following Tinboc's death. He thought it might be best to wait a couple of weeks to let folks realize that there was no plan of succession, before he took any action. Hopefully, some of the villagers would recover from the effects of Thimlomarium in that time, and Rimu would return to the mainland to tell his story of the treachery by the elder and younger Tinboc. This would probably force a new election and Tinboc's government would likely be booted out of office. Therefore, a new government would be needed and perhaps its leaders could be formed from the people of Tenaru. Rimu had decided he was too old to do all the travel and administration needed to create a new government and deal with the other civilizations, but perhaps Hanish could be elected and provide the necessary energy.

Shortly later, the attention turned toward me. I would learn that Rimu and Hanish had thought a lot more about my situation than I had. I assumed that if I wished, Rimu would send me back to my time. But that had become complicated when he told me that I was damaged in my time. Did I even want to go back? But Rimu's plan was substantially different.

"Al", Rimu began, "the decision will be yours, but I think you have several options that you will want to consider. Let us list the options we have thought about for you to consider, and you will, perhaps, have other ideas. First, you can stay with us in this time and help us create a new government. Your counsel will be considered of great value. While you have barely come to know Tenaru, there is still a new world for you to discover once we get back to the mainland. Second, you can go back to the time and place that you left. But that is not advisable, since there is still a viable entity there, and that entity is you. In your previous time, you are unable to move and mostly confined to isolation. Fortunately, you have no knowledge of that while you are here with us. And of course, if you go back, you will have no memories of ever having been in our time. Indeed, I only know this because I saw some of your life through the orb. But there is a third option. It comes

about because of what I have learned from the orb when I
sent you back to clear residual Thimlomarium from your
body. You don't know this now, but in your time, your
other self has been writing an account of your time here,
and of your life there. I could see it while you were there.
This is complicated because, as part of this suggestion, I
have an agenda that I wish to see done, but it affects you
far more than me. However, you might also get something
special from this approach".

"I suggest that we send you back to fifteen years before
you left, before the time the orb brought you here. You
will have full memory of your old life up to that point, but
you will lose any memory of the fifteen years between the
time when we send you back and the time when the orb
first sent you here. Remember, you will not have formed
any memory connections beyond the time when you are
sent back. Fifteen years before you left was not chosen at
random, your wife died of cancer five years after that point.
Perhaps, if you knew to have her checked for cancer a few
years earlier, the disease could be treated and cured. It is
only a chance, but it is a chance for a new life with your
wife and son".

I was stunned. "But you said I wouldn't remember
anything"

"Let me finish", interrupted Rimu. "Remember, there
is a written account of these events". We would need to
send you back one more time to your original time to
recover a copy of the written account. I want you to
consider going back to an earlier time, but with two gifts.
One will be the written account that you will not believe
when you read it, but that contains a true story of future
times. Another present will be one of the orbs. Now wait

and let me explain. You will remember that I told you one of the orbs was given with the intent that it would go to Southland after seventy years. That is fifty-five years from now, so it is not needed here now. If I send an orb with you, it will not be needed here for nearly four hundred years. And I can recall it if necessary. It is the orb, and learning what it represents, that will convince you that the story sent with you is real. I'm quite sure that once you accept the truth of even part of the story, you will keep the orb secret. That brings us to the part that is my agenda. You should know, since I once told you, that you came here to Tenaru accidently because I was sending an orb back to a time before McMurdoc's Folly. I had hoped that I could go back myself and stop McMurdoc from causing the disaster that bears his name. But I could never figure out a way to know what I planned to do once I got there. Only accidently bringing you here and considering how to send you back made me realize that with a written record and a reason to believe that writing, there might be a way to affect the history of what was coming. I really do not know if history can be changed, or what would happen to us if it were changed. But I have decided that anything that happens to us in this current time would be better than the hundreds of years of pain and savagery after McMurdoc's Folly. You would know what is coming and when, as well as the results. What you can do to prevent it will be up to you, if it is even possible. Yet, with an orb, perhaps you will think of a way to alter that aspect of history".

Rimu continued, "There are three additional problems with this idea. I do not think anything good can come from there being two of you in one place. Since you might meet yourself at some point, years after you are sent back, it will be necessary for the orb to eliminate the damaged version of you. That could be pretty upsetting for those who care for you. Moreover, the same thing applies to your dog, River. Actually, it may not even be possible to send the dog back, since he will technically not have been born. You will meet River again some years later, just as you did before, but this River will have to remain here. And, lastly, you will have to spend some significant amount of time as your damaged self in your original time to allow you to finish writing all of the account of what has happened".

I didn't have any concern for River's care if he stayed here; Hanish and River had become good buddies anyway. But the loss of River, my best friend, would be like losing a brother. The other side of the coin was a new chance for a life with my family. I had often thought about what I might do differently if I had another chance to live my life; now I was perhaps going to get that chance. It seemed to me that Rimu's hope of altering the future was a pipe dream, but what the hell, I might give it a try if there was an opportunity. Rimu had gotten me here to Tenaru, why should he not be able to get me back to Idaho at any time we wanted. I was surprised how easy it was for me to decide the option I wanted to try. There was going to be some real sorrow at leaving both Hanish and River, but a chance to be with my family - with none of us sick or living like a vegetable – was something for which I'd have done anything. With that decision made, there were some important preparations to be made. I'd have to teach Hanish as many of River's commands as possible, and if I could learn something about using the orb, maybe one version of me would write some of the instructions in the written account Rimu kept talking about.

That night I couldn't sleep. I worried about River. Then I worried about Rimu and Hanish trying to set up a government. What if there were problems and no one to help out. Suddenly it occurred to me that there wasn't any real reason for me to go back in some big hurry. Was there some reason for wanting to get me out of the way? It was beginning to seem like once Rimu had gotten Tinboc's orb(s), he had come up with an idea to send me back to my time immediately, even before anyone was going to the mainland. I had assassinated Oceana's leader, a man I didn't know and had never met before. It was eating at me that I had killed a man with very little regret. But what if I was wrong? What if I had killed someone who was not a bad guy, and now I was being sent to a time where I would never remember that I did it, nor would I ever know the outcome of the change of the government. It was a brilliant way to accomplish a coup. I was actually glad I wasn't going to remember any of this; it looked like I might never get answers to my questions, so at least I wouldn't be constantly burdened by a nagging guilt.

About midnight, Hanish came by my hut and spent a last night with me. She seemed genuinely sad about my decision to leave Tenaru, assured me she would take care of River, and spent the rest of the night eliminating any conspiracy theories I had, as well as any reason to think. Yea, it was going to be real hard to leave here.

I mostly dreaded going into the isolation Rimu told me was waiting for me in my original time. But that seemed a small price for the chance to be with my whole family again, and, with luck, I would only need to get through the period of isolation and paralysis one time before going to a time fifteen years prior to my infamous camping trip. My whole time on Tenaru has been a period of dealing with the unknown and with seemingly impossible events. I hoped that experience, even if I didn't remember it, would serve me well when I got to my next seemingly impossible adventure. I hadn't been ready to come to Tenaru, but I was ready to chance anything to be with my family again.

Rimu and I made the final arrangements for me to leave. Hanish stayed away except when we worked with River. I got a mini-tutorial from Rimu in the use of an orb and it scared the hell out of me – no one should have this much power. We spent long hours talking about how to secure the orbs once they were retrieved from Tinboc's office safe. Rimu and I came up with a plan to rebuild old Rooka Tinboc's power grid with three orbs and then seal all three in an energy field that could not be breached except by merging the protective field with a field generated by the orb that I was taking back in time. The world would be allowed to assume that the power grid had been formed by one orb, so that the fewest number of people possible would know there was more than one orb. At the moment, that number was three: Rimu, Hanish, and me. Even Rimu would not be able to access the orbs without recalling the orb I would have. It was clear that Rimu considered the responsibilities and potential associated with the orbs to be a curse rather than a blessing for any individual, or even group of individuals. He had fifteen years experience with his orb, and he didn't want to put that burden on Hanish if she became Oceana's leader. It seemed a good plan, but the plan's weakness was in the orb I would have, nearly four hundred years in the past. I would have the curse of caring for that orb, and trying to insure its safety beyond my years. But I wouldn't know anything about the orb, unless I believed the written account that was supposed to accompany the orb and me to an earlier time. I hoped I wouldn't throw the damn thing away before I believed the writing.

Weeks passed like it was only hours, and I was ready to be sent back to my original time. Rimu would monitor my situation with his orb and try to figure out how to get a copy of whatever I was writing. That seems easier said than done, if I couldn't help, but Rimu was clever and I wouldn't put much beyond the power of the orb. The orb that I was to take with me back in time would remain on Tenaru until I was done writing and then would be sent, including a copy of the full written account, with me back even further in time. I was being asked to be a lot more trusting than was my nature; I was willingly going into isolation, unable to do almost anything, and would not have the orb or River with me. But there was no turning back now.

During my last two weeks on Tenaru, I could see vast improvement in the function and mental capacities of the people of Tenaru. Most came out to see me leave. But it was only Hanish, River, and Rimu that made it difficult to say goodbye. They were my touchstone, my reasons to believe that this amazing adventure had been real. After I said goodbye to Rimu and River, Hanish stepped up and hugged me. I wished her all the best and gave her a quick kiss. When I kissed her, she slipped something into my hand. Immediately she stepped away. The intense bright light came over me before I had a chance to even look at what I was holding.

# Postscript

Dr. Al Hart is my Dad, and I am his son, Jon. The reason I am restating the obvious will be clear in a few minutes. My Dad's story of Tenaru and the Geezer Garage is done and what is going to be written about that has been written. I felt it necessary for me to add a few words before letting anyone else read this, to tie up a few loose ends.

As I mentioned at the beginning of this account, I came back to Idaho, with the repaired computer, to be with my Dad. I had hope that he would continue writing his story from the time the computer keyboard broke, and more importantly, that we could communicate through the computer. I would write a message to him and when he typed, he might be able to respond to me.

It was a revelation for both Dad and me when we first exchanged messages. For almost a full month we exchanged stories, requests, and discussion about his story. His mind was clear as a bell, and he remembered everything about the stories he had written that talked of events before the camping trip, but nothing about Tenaru, except what he had read. We wrote each other about his situation and his prognosis; the latter wasn't too hopeful since it included Carpel Tunnel syndrome in his left wrist and the beginning of rheumatoid arthritis in both hands. What the assisted living facility could do for him was to manage any pain and wait for a medical breakthrough that might help him. Dad clearly understood this and was uncharacteristically upbeat for someone in his situation. He kept bringing our discussion back to whether I believed if what he had written about Tenaru could be more than a dream. I didn't want to put a damper on his hopes, but it just seemed too amazing to me, so I danced around a definitive answer. At least I did until last week.

Before I got back to Idaho, my Dad had been unresponsive. He typed as he did almost every day, and the staff moved him around as usual, but he remained "in his own world", as one staffer said. So one day when he was set up at the computer table, the staff member was surprised to find a piece of cloth folded up in his hand. It was addressed to Al Hart, and sealed with a pitch-like substance. Since I had notified the geezer garage that I was returning, she put it aside to give to me. It was just assumed that Dad couldn't open it or wouldn't be able to read or understand it; both assumptions were incorrect, by the way. But the cloth was forgotten until the second week I was there. They gave it to me as I was leaving one evening. At Dad's house, where I was staying, I pried off the sealing material and read the letter written on it.

The next ten days were a flurry of activity for me and of intense thought by my Dad. The letter, written by Hanish, gave us a series of instructions, and asked my Dad for certain preparations. I followed the instructions and worked with my Dad on the preparations. All this time, as I fulfilled the requests of the letter, I thought about how someone else might have written this letter and signed Hanish's name. A few of the staff at the facility could have read my Dad's account, but none had ever said a word about it to me. But the letter was written on a green cloth-like material that I'd never seen before. Dad couldn't have done the things asked for in the letter by himself; either it was a good thing I had come to see him when I did, or Hanish knew much more than I could comprehend. Anyway that I looked at it, this letter was more than just a coincidence.

This is what the letter on the green material said:

"Dearest Al,

The accident that brought you to Tenaru was the best thing to happen in my life. Please know that I understand your decision to leave to be with your family, yet I am happy we had our time together. Still, it will take me some time to get over my loss. But, as you will see, I shall be frightfully busy soon enough.

The task at hand is to prepare you for your trip back to be with your family. You will not be coming back to Tenaru, but back instead to before your wife was ill. Please see that these requests are done as quickly as possible. First, finish what you have not yet written. Second, have copies made of the written account. Make electronic copies and at least one paper copy. These must be connected to your body before we send you back. If any copies are left behind when you leave, remove the description of the orb and how it is used. Third, think what you will need to take with you in order to read the electronic version of the written account (your computer is too new), and if there is anything else you must have with you when you go back. Fourth, prepare your son because, when you leave, you will cease to exist in your present state and it could be upsetting. Fifth, keep this letter on you when you prepare to leave.

I have decided to run for Prime Minister of Oceana, with my Dad's support, once our people are well and we can return to the mainland. You will probably not be surprised to know that Rimu has been planning my position in government for years; however, because of you, the chance may come more quickly than any of us thought. Moreover, don't be surprised when I bring you back here sometime in the future, so you can see that we are indeed building something good.     But there is another important reason.

I am pregnant with your child. In a number of months, you will have two children, one in your time, and one in mine. If it is a boy, it will be named Al. I am planning for these two siblings to meet when next you return here. I wish you all the best!

Love, Hanish".

My Dad was beside himself, at least as much as one can be on paper (actually on the computer). He was sure he would soon be on another adventure and out of the Geezer Garage, with the chance of returning to see the folks of Tenaru at some point in the future. He wrote repeatedly telling me to be happy for him. He said he had little hope to be much use or help to me in his current state, but if his story was correct, he had another chance to be a better Dad and perhaps change the course of history leading up to McMurdoc's Folly. He told me not to worry about him any more. We would both be in better places soon. He would miss me as he knew me now, but he thought he had an opportunity now to be a better Dad to me in the past.

What was I suppose to think? Are there multiple time-lines where my Dad can be living now, where he can be living 400 years in the future, and where he can be living fifteen years in the past? All while I am living in the only time I know. I wish I could answer these questions. All I could do was put the stuff Dad wanted in a bag and fasten it around his wrist each night.

But I do know that my Dad disappeared from the Geezer Garage four days ago. When I came into the facility and went to my Dad's room, he wasn't there. When I asked about him, no one knew where he was. Several of us searched the facility, but he was not to be found. Finally, the Director of the Geezer Garage came to talk to me and told me, in front of several staff, that my Dad had been taken to the hospital. That turned out to be a fabrication made up to buy more time to find my Dad. It turns out that he wasn't in any hospital for miles around. Dr. Al Hart had just disappeared. How does an elder care facility lose a patient who can't move?

The story of my Dad's disappearance made the local, then national, news, and as a result, a lawyer representing the Geezer Garage contacted me. It seems that if I am willing not to sue the facility, I will receive a significant monetary settlement. I guess my Dad was right; it looks like we may both be in a better place after all.

I know now what I have chosen to believe of my Dad's story. I'm looking forward to meeting my new brother or sister.

# ABOUT THE AUTHOR

Dr. Bill Trumble spent most of his professional career as a Professor, medical researcher, university administrator and President of a small biotechnology company. He now lives in Redmond, Oregon with his wife, cat, and memory of his favorite dog, River.